Praise for SAVING RED

A YALSA Quick Pick for Reluctant Young Adult Readers Book
A Texas TAYSHAS Title

"This tender, taut novel in verse is both wise and full of heart."
—Deb Caletti, National Book Award finalist

"A beautiful window into the desperate futility of trying to
save someone who doesn't necessarily want to be saved."
—ALA *Booklist* (starred review)

"Original. Heart-wrenching. A beautiful treatise on
empathy and love. These characters belong to you—as your own friends—
when you read their story. *Saving Red* is an absolute treasure."
—John Corey Whaley, Printz Award winner &
National Book Award finalist

"Each carefully crafted poem comes together to paint a vivid
picture of love, loss, and the hope and humor that's caught in between.
Saving Red soars and will speak to the hearts of teen readers everywhere."
—Dr. Rose Brock, Sam Houston State University

"A quick, accessible read for fans of emotional, character-driven titles."
—*SLJ*

"Sones's staccato, first-person poems sensitively trace
the innocence Molly sheds as her world expands."
—*Publishers Weekly*

Praise for STOP PRETENDING:
WHAT HAPPENED WHEN MY BIG SISTER WENT CRAZY

A YALSA Quick Pick for Reluctant Young Adult Readers Book
An ALA Popular Paperbacks for Young Adults Book
A Christopher Award Winner
An ALA Best Fiction for Young Adults Book
An IRA/CBC Young Adults' Choice

"The poems have a cumulative emotional power."
—ALA *Booklist* (starred review)

"Heartfelt." —*KLIATT* (starred review)

"The poems take on life and movement,
the individual frames of a movie that in the unspooling
become animated, telling a compelling tale."
—*Kirkus Reviews*

"Unpretentious. Accessible. Deeply felt."
—*SLJ*

"Sensitively written."
—*The Horn Book*

"This debut novel shows the capacity of poetry to record the personal and
translate it into the universal."
—*Chicago Tribune*

"*Stop Pretending* is a tour de force debut. It celebrates truth-telling and has a purity
and passion that speaks to the heart."
—*Boston Globe*

THE OPPOSITE OF INNOCENT

SONYA SONES

Quill Tree Books
An Imprint of HarperCollinsPublishers

Also by Sonya Sones:

Stop Pretending
What My Mother Doesn't Know
One of Those Hideous Books Where the Mother Dies
What My Girlfriend Doesn't Know
To Be Perfectly Honest
Saving Red

Quill Tree Books is an imprint of HarperCollins Publishers.

The Opposite of Innocent
information address HarperCollins Children's Books, a division of
HarperCollins Publishers, 195 Broadway, New York, NY 10007.
www.epicreads.com

Library of Congress Control Number: 2018939978
ISBN 978-0-06-237032-7

Typography by Catherine San Juan
21 22 23 24 25 PC/LSCH 10 9 8 7 6 5 4 3 2 1

❖

First paperback edition, 2021

For all the Lilys . . .

The Friend of the Family

I've always been in love
with Luke.

For as far back
as I can remember.

I used to climb into his lap,
throw my arms around his neck,

and tell him I was gonna marry him
when I grew up.

And Luke would smile down at me
and say,

"I'll wait for you, Lily.
I promise."

It's Been Two Endless Years

Since he left for Kenya.
But today—
he's finally coming back.

When Luke left,
I was flat as an ironing board.
Now I'm more like an ironing board with boobs.

When Luke left, I had a billion zits.
Now I've only got a million.
Plus, I've mastered the magic of makeup.

When Luke left, my mouth was so full of braces
it felt like my teeth were wrapped
in barbed wire.

Yesterday I got them off.
Now my teeth feel smoother
than my iPhone screen.

I can't stop running my tongue over them.
I've been smiling so much my cheeks hurt.
And everyone's been smiling back.

When Luke Left

I felt like
a caterpillar.

Like
this blobby

thing
waiting to happen.

Now
I feel more like a butterfly—

a butterfly who can't decide
which wings to wear.

I've Tried On Everything in My Closet

Twice.
I've rifled through all my drawers.
I've even braved the spidery depths
beneath my bed.

But it's no use—it's all too old
or tight or loose, or just plain ugly.
I text Taylor and Rose for emergency
wardrobe advice, but they don't text back.

Then I hear my little sister Alice
clomping down the stairs in my shoes.
She's always playing dress-up with my stuff
and "forgetting" to return it.

I dash down the hall and dig through her drawers
till I find my clingy pink top—the one that's been
missing so long I figured I'd left it at Rose's
after one of our sleepovers.

I race back to my room to put it on.
I shimmy into my favorite jeans,
swipe on some Kiss Me Quick lip gloss,
and pause to study myself in the mirror.

How will I look to Luke?
Will he notice how much I've changed?
Have I changed as much
as I think I have?

Then Mom's Shouting

She's saying we have to leave right now
or we won't be there when Luke's plane lands.
But I haven't started on my hair yet . . .
I'm not even close to ready!

I rake my fingers through my crazed curls,
then heave a sigh.
Oh, who am I kidding?
I'll never be ready.

"Lily," Mom shouts. "I'm counting to ten.
One . . . two . . . three . . ."
"Wow," I shout back.
"You're so good at that."

I grab the point-and-shoot camera
Luke gave me on my eighth birthday,
flip open the jewelry box
he gave me on my tenth,

and search for the gold earrings
he gave me on my twelfth,
just before he went to Kenya.
I slip them on and dash down the stairs.

Dad's standing by the door, sending a text.
I ask him how I look.
He says, "Great . . ." without even glancing up.
It sucks. But I'm used to it.

Driving to the Airport

Mom's sitting next to Dad
and I'm in back with Alice,
beating my curls into submission.

Alice is squirmier than a puppy,
chanting, "We're gonna see Luke!
We're gonna see Luke!"

Which would probably
be totally annoying
if she were some other little kid.

But she's Alice.
And those pink cheeks of hers,
that halo of golden curls—

well, it's sort of like having
an actual angel for a sister.
And it's not just her looks.

I swear to God, the kid's got a sixth sense.
She's only six, but she always knows if I'm sad.
Even when I'm trying to hide it.

And once she decides I need some cheering up,
she'll cross her eyes till she's half-blind
if she thinks it'll help.

Not That I'm a Particularly Sad Person

I'm basically pretty upbeat.
Mom says I was born that way.
She claims I popped out of her womb,
and instead of crying, I said,
"Whoa! That was amazing!"

Though when Luke left,
I felt like I'd lost a limb or something.
He was so deep in the rain forest,
searching for a cure for malaria,
we couldn't even text or talk on the phone.

I missed the sound of his voice.
That beautiful English accent of his . . .
Mom was too sad to even notice how sad *I* was.
And as usual, Dad worked late most nights,
or just sat in front of the TV watching sports.

But Alice
never left my side—
putting on "ballet recitals" for me,
prancing around in her tutu nonstop,
doing her best to distract me.

And whenever I got a little weepy,
she'd pop my camera into my hands,
telling me she needed a new head shot.
And as soon as I started snapping away,
I'd begin to feel better.

Suddenly

Alice spots the first sign for the airport
and ramps up her chanting:
"Luke! Luke! Luke! Luke! Luke!"

Now it *is* totally annoying.
I can't go on like this much longer.
I yank my camera out of my pocket.

It's pretty beat up,
but it still works fine.
And it makes me feel more like . . .

Well, more like a serious artist, I guess,
than when I just use
my cell phone camera.

I focus my lens on Alice and say,
"Stop chanting. I wanna get a picture of you
without your mouth open."

"You're not the boss of me," she says.
But then she flashes her most angelic smile.
The kid could win a cuteness contest. Seriously.

It was Alice who got me into photography.
She was such an adorable baby, I just *had*
to take her picture. Pretty much all the time.

And then I started taking pictures of everything else.

In Baggage Claim

My heart's thumping like crazy
as I stare down the long hallway,
trying to spot Luke in the crowd.

I feel like maybe I'm gonna swoon—
like I'm the heroine of one of those
love stories I'm always reading.

And as I wait for my first glimpse of him,
my whole life seems
to hold

its breath . . .

Then—There He Is

Waving at us and smiling,
looking tan and sort of lumberjack-ish.

And even more beautiful
than I remember.

I snap a photo,
to try to capture it.

Then Alice is slipping her hand into mine,
whispering, "He's home."

And Luke's rushing over,
pulling my parents into a hug.

Was he always
that much taller than Dad?

Now he's lifting Alice right off her feet,
swinging her around.

And now he's swinging her
back down to earth,

reaching for me, saying, "Lily . . . My Lily . . .
You turned into a woman while I was gone!"

Oh my *God*.

And Then

Luke's
wrapping his arms
around me.

And for a few seconds,
while my cheek's pressed
against his heart,

everything is perfect.

Luke Slings His Luggage into the Trunk

While I stand close to him—
so that when he climbs into the backseat,
I can slide in right next to him.
I picture his thigh
resting against mine,
and my heart floats up into my throat.

But when he reaches for the door handle,
Mom shoos his fingers away,
saying, "Your legs are too long.
I can sit with the girls."
Alice begs to sit on Luke's lap,
but Mom tells her that wouldn't be safe.

Alice scowls and flings herself onto the backseat.
I follow her in and put my arm around her shoulder.
Mom slips in last, and says,
"You'll have plenty of time to sit on Luke's lap.
He'll be staying with us till he finds a place."
"He will?" Alice and I cry in unison.

"I will!" Luke says.
And as we head home, with Alice babbling
about all the ballet recitals she'll do for him,
I just sit here snapping pictures
of his long brown hair fluttering in the breeze,
wishing I could weave my fingers through it.

Luke Will Be Sleeping in the Guest Room

Right next to mine!
I'm listening to him unpack, opening and
closing drawers, whistling to himself,

while I lie here on my bed, swiping through
all the photos I took of him today.
Of his hair. His arms. His hands . . .

Then I get a text from Taylor:
Forgive me! Was in mid-experiment.
Available for wardrobe consult now!

(Taylor's away at chemistry camp.)
I reply: Crisis averted. Then I add a smiley face,
so it won't seem like I'm mad.

I go back to looking at photos of Luke.
Of his dark eyes. His dizzying smile . . .
Then I get a text from Rose:

Sorry I couldn't answer before!
Was busy saving a gorgeous guy's life!
U still need help?

(Rose is in Cape Cod, being a junior lifeguard.)
I reply: No problem! Figured it out. Then I
set my phone to silent. I mean, I love my besties.

But can't they see I'm busy?

Dinner

Luke's sitting between Mom and Alice.
I chose to sit next to Dad, right across from them,
so I could gaze at Luke's face in the candlelight.

Alice is telling him
she doesn't want him to find an apartment.
She wants him to live with us forever.

Luke is laughing,
saying he's pretty sure
that would be overstaying his welcome.

And that English accent of his . . .
It makes him sound like he stepped
straight out of the pages of one of my books . . .

He says he's got a month before
he has to start writing up his research results
for the foundation that sent him to Kenya.

He says he'll use that time to look for a place.
But Mom says there's no hurry.
And Dad says we've got plenty of room.

And all the while,
Luke's eyes are smiling
into mine.

I'm Imagining Him Standing Up

And coming around to my side of the table
to take my hand and whisk me off to Hawaii,
just like Olly does with Maddy
in *Everything, Everything* . . .

Then, all of a sudden,
I notice that everyone's laughing.
And when I look around the table,
I realize they're laughing at *me*.

Oh man . . .
I can feel my cheeks turning pinker
than the cherry pie Mom baked.
"What . . . ?" I say.

"Luke asked you a question, Lily," Dad says.
"Oh . . . ," I say. "I knew that."
Which makes them all laugh
even harder.

"Lily's always been a daydreamer," Luke says.
"That's one of the things we love about her, right?"
And everyone agrees,
while I sit here trying not to faint.

Because Luke just said he loves things about me!

It's August

So it's still too warm to light a fire.

But after dessert, Mom carries the candles
from the dinner table into the living room,
and then lights a few more.

Now the candlelight
flickers on our faces,
as I sit here at Luke's feet,

listening to him tell about
the time he was attacked by a leopard,
deep in the Kenyan rain forest—

about how he had to shove
his forearm into its mouth
to keep it from lunging for his neck.

And while it shook him around like a rag doll,
he somehow managed to pull out his pistol
and shoot it dead.

Then Luke rolls up his shirtsleeve
to show us where the leopard's teeth
sank in.

And when I see those rough red scars,
when I see how close he came to being killed,
my heart turns over.

Luke Says It's Time for Presents

He gives Dad a Maasai spear
decorated with bloodred charms.
It looks like it could do some serious damage.
"My only request," Luke says,
"is that you promise not to use it on *me*, Sam."
My father laughs and fakes a lunge at him.

Then Luke gives Mom a handwoven blue blanket,
and says, "It matches your eyes, Julia."
Mom blushes like a seventh grader.
Next, Luke gives Alice a set of wooden animals.
He says they're called "the Great Five"—a lion,
a buffalo, an elephant, a rhino, and a leopard.

"I love them!" she cries.
But she hands him back the leopard,
saying, "This one is *not* so great."
Luke smiles and pats her on the head.
"It's not the one that bit me, luv," he says,
tucking it into her palm.

Finally, he places a small box into *my* hands.
Inside is the prettiest necklace I've ever seen—
each green jewel more sparkly than the next.
"The stones are called tsavorite," Luke says.
And as he fastens it around my neck,
he whispers in my ear,

"Tsavorite for my favorite."

Luke's Always Given Alice and Me

The best presents ever.
Even when it wasn't our birthdays.
It's like he knows what we want before we do.
Unlike Dad, who never gives us presents.
Even when it *is* our birthday.

Though it's not because he's cheap.
It's because he's got to work such long hours
at his tech start-up company
that he hardly spends any time with us.
So he doesn't really know what we'd like.

Mom works too, at an art gallery,
but only nine to three.
Dad works nine to infinity.
And when he comes home, he's too tired
to do anything but sit in front of a screen.

That's why Mom does all the gift buying,
and the wrapping, too.
Then they both sign the card.
But it's obvious from the look on Dad's face
while we're unwrapping the boxes,

that he doesn't even know what's inside them.

It's After Midnight

I'm lying in bed, wearing my pj's
and Luke's necklace,

remembering the thrill
that ran through me like water

when his lips
brushed against my ear . . .

Luke's bedroom and mine share a wall.
Both of our beds touch that wall.

I draw a heart on it
with the tip of my finger,

imagining Luke doing the same thing
on *his* side of the wall.

I press my palm against
its skin-smooth surface.

Is Luke pressing his palm against it, too?
Are our fingers almost

touching?

My Parents Have to Work

So Luke's been spending the last few
weeks of summer with Alice and me.
Alice calls it Camp Luke-a-Wanna.
Today we're at the U-Pick-Em Apple Farm.

The trees sag under the weight
of an early crop, redder than valentines.
The bees hum as we twist the apples
off their stems and drop them into our sacks.

Luke notices that Alice is too short
to reach all but the lowest branches.
So he lets her ride on his shoulders.
Because that's the kind of guy he is.

Alice grins and raises her arms
over her head like a ballerina.
And as I snap her picture,
I can't help wishing I was *her* size . . .

We take a break from apple picking.
Alice dances off after a dragonfly.
Luke leads me over to sit under one of the trees.
He shines an apple on the leg of his faded jeans.

He takes a bite, then passes it to me.
And as he watches me bring it to my lips,
I can't help thinking how very
Adam-and-Eve-ish this moment is.

At the Cineplex

Alice wanted to see the new *Ice Age* movie.
And I don't blame her—I was obsessed
with those films at her age, too.

Of course, I lost interest in them years ago.
But even so, there's no place
I'd rather be right now

than sitting here
in the delicious dark
next to Luke,

listening
to the sound of his laughter
rumbling all through him,

his forearm
resting tinglingly close
to mine.

And when he reaches into my lap
to dig a handful of popcorn
out of the bag,

my breath catches.

Because the Truth Is

No guy's ever reached into my lap before.
Not for popcorn or for anything else.
A few have tried to kiss me.
But I just ducked out of the way.

Because compared to Luke,
they all seemed so immature.
Though I did let this guy named Jason
kiss me after a school dance last year.

I barely even knew him,
but I was getting tired of listening
to Taylor and Rose swap stories about
all the boys they'd been making out with.

Tired
of being the one
who'd never been
kissed.

Jason's breath smelled like beer.
His tongue was thick and slimy.
I almost gagged when he pushed it
into my mouth.

I mean, I don't understand how exchanging saliva
with someone can feel so weirdly . . . impersonal.
There has to be more to it than that.
There just *has* to be.

Alice Lobbied Hard for Bowling

So today Luke's taking us
to Looking Glass Lanes—
one of those places that's geared
toward little kids, with balls that weigh
less than cotton candy, and bumpers
that keep them out of the gutter.

When we walk through the door,
Alice starts twirling around,
crying, "We're in Wonderland!"
Luke grins at her and says,
"Everywhere is Wonderland
when we're with you, Alice."

He tousles her curls,
and just as I raise my camera,
to capture this moment between them,
he looks over at me,
and gives me a secret wink.
My knees go all wobbly.

Then,
for the next few hours,
Luke cheers Alice and me on
like we're Olympic champions,
even when we just knock over a few pins.
Everywhere is Wonderland

when we're with Luke.

But When We're with Dad

Everywhere
is more like
I-Wonder-Why-Not-Land.

Alice and I
came here with *him*
last summer.

But he didn't cheer us on.
He mostly just stared at his phone
till it was his turn again.

I'm making him sound like
a much worse father than he actually is.
He's not that bad.

It's just that he doesn't know
how to relate to Alice and me.
He doesn't seem comfortable around us.

Like he thinks
we're these delicate crystals
that might break if he looks at us sideways.

Which probably explains why he never hugs us.
Or maybe that's just a story
I made up in my head

to let him off the hook.

Because I Do Love Him

And, I mean,
it's probably not even his fault
that he is like he is.

Mom's theory is that his parents
never used to hug *him*—so he just figures
that's how people are supposed to be.

He doesn't
hug Mom either.
At least not in front of us.

I wish I'd gotten to meet his parents.
But they died in a car crash, with his little brother,
when Dad was just a freshman in college.

Mom thinks that's why he wanted
to get married and start a family
before they even graduated—

to replace the one he'd lost.

And I'm Pretty Sure He Doesn't Regret It

I can tell by how
he sneaks into my room at night
when he thinks I'm asleep,

how he tucks the blankets around me,
and rests his hand on my forehead,
like he's checking to see if I have a fever.

And Alice says
he does the same thing
to her.

It's so strange—like he can only
show us how he really feels about us
when he thinks we aren't looking.

My dad may be messed up,
but I'm pretty sure he loves us.
And we love him back.

I just sometimes wish
he could act more
like Luke.

Luke's Been My Dad's Best Friend Forever

They both went to the same university.
Dad was working as a teaching assistant
to help pay his way through grad school.

And when Luke was a freshman,
he enrolled in one of Dad's classes.
They started hanging out right away.

Even though Dad was like five years older.
Mom thinks it's because Luke sort of filled the hole
left in Dad's life when his little brother died.

And Luke's family lived in London,
where he was raised, so my parents
kind of became his American family.

It's weird to think that Luke was already
fifteen years old when I was born—
a year older than I am now.

He used to babysit for me all the time.
I cringe whenever I think
about that.

I mean, he used to change my diapers
and give me baths.
Luke has seen me *naked*.

I was only a toddler, but still.

If You've Just Done the Math in Your Head

Then I can guess
what you're thinking.
Something along the lines of:

"Wait. *What?*
You mean Luke's twenty-nine?
That's practically *thirty*."

But
lots of couples
have big age differences.

And I mean, girls fall in love
with their teachers all the time.
This is no different than that.

You'd
understand
why I'm so into Luke . . .

You'd understand how . . .
how epically . . . epic he is,
if you knew him

like I do.

For Example:

When I was
four years old,
I choked on an M&M.

I tried to call for help,
but no sound
would come out.

It was Luke who found me
a few seconds later
and told me to sit up,

Luke who thwacked me on my back,
and made that M&M
fly out of my mouth,

Luke who clutched me to his chest
and murmured, "Lily . . . my Lily . . ."
over and over again.

It was Luke
who rescued me.
Luke.

When I Was Seven

My dad's tech start-up
almost went under.

This big corporation sued him
or something.

My parents
never explained why.

They just said that unless a miracle happened,
we were gonna go bankrupt.

But then,
a miracle *did* happen.

Luke
happened.

He'd just inherited
a bunch of money from his grandfather.

So he invested most of it
in Dad's company

and saved the day.

When I Was Ten

Luke moved into a place
that was literally around the corner.
He'd always lived in the same city as us,
studying for his doctorate, and then working.
So we used to see him at least once a week.

But now
that he lived so close,
he came over all the time.
It made every day
feel like Christmas.

Dad was too late for dinner most nights.
But Luke was always there—
helping Mom cook,
teaching us old English whaling songs,
showing us how to make shepherd's pie.

Then, while Mom gave Alice a bath
and put her to bed, he'd help me with my homework.
Afterwards, he'd sit with me on the couch,
put his arm around my shoulder, and ask me how I was.
Like he actually wanted to know the answer.

So I poured my heart out to him.
I told him things I couldn't tell anyone else.
And he listened. I mean really listened.
He was my best friend, my hero,
and my soul mate all rolled into one.

He Was Sort of Like a Character from a Novel

A novel I couldn't put down.
I love reading almost as much as I love Luke.
When I'm under the spell of a book,
it's like I'm living in its pages.

I look at my face in the mirror,
and see the heroine's eyes staring back at me.
And when I put my hand over my chest,
I feel *her* heart beating.

I especially love *love* stories.
Rose and I both do.
It was love stories
that brought us together.

We met each other
in Bella's Bookshop,
just before the beginning
of seventh grade.

When Bella introduced us,
we ended up talking for three hours straight
about which Jane Austen novel
was the most romantic.

Rose: definitely *Pride and Prejudice*.
Me: definitely *Persuasion*.
But it didn't matter.
Because we'd already become best friends.

And Books Aren't *All* We Have in Common

Both our moms apparently
thought it would be adorable
to name us after flowers.

And we both knew, when Taylor
showed up on the first day of school,
that our circle had been completed.

We arranged to meet for lunch in the cafeteria,
and got so busy talking,
we forgot to eat.

Taylor's stories about
blowing stuff up at chemistry camp
made us laugh so hard we nearly peed.

By the end of the day,
Taylor started calling us
"the Triatomics."

Rose and I had to Google it.
Turns out a triatomic is a single molecule
made of three different atoms.

Which is exactly
what it feels like we've been
ever since.

This Morning

Alice and I are apartment hunting with Luke.
I hate the thought of him moving out,
but it's sorta fun to see all the different places.

In each apartment the agent shows us,
I imagine what it would be like
to live there with Luke.

What it would be like
to cook dinner together
in the shiny new kitchen.

What it would be like
to hold hands on the balcony,
watching the sunset.

What it would be like
to take a bath with him
in the extra-deep jetted tub.

What
it would
be *like* . . .

But then the agent says,
"You could convert this den into a bedroom
for these two darling kids of yours."

And my imaginings grind to a screeching halt.

The Next Day, It's Pouring Out

So we decide to have a stay-at-home
Camp Luke-a-Wanna day.
He teaches us how to play
a game called Sardines:

One person hides and the others search for him.
Then, as each person finds him,
they squeeze into the hiding place with him.
And the last person to find the others is the loser.

Luke hides first,
in a tiny closet tucked under the stairs.
It only takes me a few minutes to locate him.
I wriggle in next to him.

Now, as we wait for Alice to find us,
sitting here together in the thrilling dark,
Luke's thigh is pressed against mine,
his fingers resting lightly on my ankle.

Our heads are so close
I can feel his breath on my neck.
My heart's beating so loud
I'm afraid he'll hear it.

Or worse still—
that Alice will.
Because I really don't want her
to find us.

But, of Course, She *Does*

Just a few
all-too-short minutes
later.

When she swings open the closet door
and finds us huddled inside,
she squeals with delight.

And as Luke climbs out,
I could swear I hear him
mutter, "Damn . . ."

Though I probably
just imagined it.
I'm sure I imagined it.

He Holds Out Both Hands to Help Me Up

Then he laces our fingers together.
"Would you like to hide next, Lily?" he says.
And his voice vibrates all through me.

He's looking right into my eyes when he asks.
And I'm so flustered I can't speak.
So I just nod.

But Alice breaks the spell.
"No more Sardines," she says.
"It gets too lonely when I'm the only one left."

A cloud passes over Luke's face.
Though it comes and goes so fast,
I'm not even sure if it was ever there.

"Let's have a ballet recital instead," Alice says.
He shoots her a look.
Then he turns back to me with a shrug,

and unlaces our fingers.

I've Been Wearing Luke's Necklace 24/7

And every night,
I've fallen asleep
with my fingers resting
on its smooth green stones.

I've only taken it off
when I'm in the tub.
Which is where I am right now,
up to my neck in creamy bubbles.

But my fingers are starting to shrivel
and Mom's shouting that dinner's in ten.
So I sigh myself out of the water,
and towel off.

I look at my face in the mirror.
My cheeks are flushed from soaking in the tub.
Or maybe from that deeply sudsy daydream
I just had about Luke.

I slip on my bathrobe,
fasten the clasp on my necklace,
tug open the bathroom door—
and bump right into him!

I Mean, Like I Literally Bump Right into Him

I grab my forehead
where it collided with his collarbone,
and we both take a quick step back.

"Sorry!" I say.
"You all right?" he asks, letting his dark eyes
travel quickly over my body.

I glance down
and realize that my bathrobe
has fallen open.

I yank it shut as Luke's eyes meet mine,
and the flush on my cheeks
spreads to the rest of me.

Then Luke smiles this funny little smile and says,
"You really *have* become a woman, Lily—
a gorgeous one . . ."

Oh my *God*.
My mouth goes so dry I can't even speak.
So I just flash Luke my braces-free smile

and dash down the hall to my room.

I Close the Door Behind Me

And lean against it,
feeling strangely breathless,
as Luke's words echo all through me.
"Five-minute warning," Mom calls.

So I pull myself together,
slip on my slinky black lace top,
pour myself into my favorite jeans,
and swipe on some lip gloss.

A second later,
as I float down the stairs,
I hear Luke's door opening,
his footsteps following right behind mine.

A sweet shiver runs through me.
I can feel his eyes on me.
Feel them taking in
every single inch of me.

But I'm an Idiot

Because when
I reach the bottom step
and turn around,

I see that he's not
even looking at me.
He's looking at his phone.

He's all dressed up—
his hair slicked back,
wearing a fancy sports coat,

and he must have
some kind of aftershave on,
because he smells like the woods.

He pockets his phone, then tells Mom
he's meeting an old friend for dinner.
"An old girlfriend's more like it," Dad laughs.

Then Luke kisses Mom's cheek
and says, "Good night, kids," waving
in the general direction of Alice and me.

But he never even glances at me.
And when the door closes behind him,
it feels like all the air in the house

has followed him out into the street.

Now I Know

I know that even though Luke said
I've turned into a woman,

he still thinks of me
as a child.

Less than an hour ago,
I'd convinced myself

that some kind of magic
had happened.

That Luke had stayed the same age
while I grew up.

That he'd waited
for me.

Just like he promised me he would
when I was a little girl.

I Just Googled It

And found out
that when you love someone
in an all-consuming way,

even though it makes no sense
because you know that person
doesn't love you back,

and you know for sure
that there's absolutely no chance
of him *ever* loving you back

because
you'll always be
way too young for him,

but you keep on
loving that person
anyway,

and thinking about them
every minute of every day—
that's called obsessive love.

And I'm pretty sure
I've got the world's
worst case of it.

Sometimes

Sometimes
I feel like a book.

Like a book
that's never been opened—

hidden away
in a long-forgotten library,

waiting for someone
to find me,

ease me off
my shelf,

and read me.

It's Saturday

And Dad has actually decided
to take a day off for once.

So Alice and I have to share Luke
with him and Mom.

Alice wanted
to feed the ducks.

So we packed some sandwiches (for us)
and some stale bread (for the ducks).

Now we're strolling along
the dirt path next to the river,

headed for a picnic near the little cove
where the ducks hang out.

Luke and Dad are walking up ahead of us,
talking in low tones.

Luke must be telling him
how his date went last night.

My stomach turns over
just thinking about it.

Obsessive love sucks.

I Don't Want to Eavesdrop on Dad and Luke

I really don't.
But the breeze
keeps blowing their words
back to me.

"Amber?" Dad says. "Wasn't she the one
who followed you around campus like a puppy?"
"Yeah," Luke says with a chuckle.
"The girl just wouldn't take no for an answer."

Dad bursts out laughing at this.
"You've never said no to a girl in your life."
"She *was* a hot little thing," Luke says.
"But she's even hotter now—aged, like fine wine."

Just then,
Mom puts on some speed to catch up to them,
and slips her arm through Luke's.
All talk of Amber comes to a sudden halt.

"Hey," Alice cries, "wait for me!"
She runs up and takes hold of Luke's other hand.
Leaving me alone, to scuff along behind them,
kicking every stone and pebble in my path.

My Phone Buzzes in My Pocket

It's a text from Rose to Taylor and me:
Sleepover 2nite. My house. 7?
Taylor texts right back:
No place I'd rather be.
Except maybe in a lab.
Or anywhere with Channing Tatum. ☺

They just got back
from Cape Cod and chemistry camp.
(I still can't believe Taylor went there *voluntarily*.)
I've missed them both to pieces.
But I wouldn't be very good company . . .
What should I say?

Rose texts again: Say YES, Lil.
Whoa . . . Sometimes I think that girl
can actually read my mind.
And Taylor adds:
Don't u wanna hear all our
racy tales of summer romance?

Which is when I finally cave:
I totally do. I'll bring the popcorn.
And Rose texts back: Thank goodness!
Cuz we gotta discuss The Sky Is Everywhere
+ whether Lennie shud have given her heart
to Toby or to Joe!!!

What would I do without those two?

Saturday Night

I've thrown my pj's,
my toothbrush, and a bag of popcorn
into my backpack.

A second ago, I said goodbye to Dad.
But he was so busy watching a football game
he didn't even notice.

Sometimes he makes me feel
like I'm the least important
person on the planet.

Now I'm waiting by the front door
while Mom searches her purse
for her car keys.

Alice is doing a "goodbye ballet" for me,
pirouetting her little heart out,
when Luke comes trotting down the stairs.

He's all dressed up to go out again.
That's two nights in a row now.
But who's counting? Sigh . . .

He stops short when he sees me standing here
with my backpack slung over my shoulder,
and offers to give me a lift.

He offers to give me a lift!

What Is It About Being Alone in a Car?

Alone
in a car at sunset
with the guy you're obsessively
in love with?

Is it the soft leather seats?
The dim dashboard light?
The jazz oozing
out of the speakers?

Or is it how his hands
guiding the steering wheel
are so ridiculously beautiful
you wish you could photograph them?

What is it about being
alone in this car with Luke right now,
that's making me feel
like my whole body's humming,

right along with the engine?

Suddenly Luke's Laughing

And I don't
have any idea why.
"What's . . . so funny?" I say.

"Well," he says,
"I just asked you something,
and I've got a feeling you didn't hear me."

"Oh," I say. "Sorry . . .
I must have been . . . I guess I was—"
"Daydreaming again?" Luke says.

And then he flashes me a smile
that's so . . . so . . . Well it's just so *loving*,
that I probably would have keeled right over.

I mean,
if I weren't already
sitting down.

As We Turn Left onto Kingsley

Luke says, "I'll repeat the question:
Who's going to be there tonight?"
"Oh," I say. "Just Rose and Taylor."

"Tell me about them," he says.
And my heart skips a little beat,
because he actually seems interested.

"Well . . . Rose is sort of an adventurer," I say.
"And she's really into reading love stories, like me.
So we never run out of stuff to talk about."

"And Taylor?" Luke asks.
"Tay?" I say. "Tay's an amazing scientist, like you.
And the funniest, coolest guy in the whole school."

"Did you say 'guy'?" Luke asks.
"Yeah," I say with a shrug. "He's awesome.
No one makes me laugh like him."

Luke furrows his brow and says,
"Sounds like you really fancy this chap."
And I'm not even sure why,

but instead of telling him the truth—
that Taylor's one hundred percent gay—
I just smile in a secret sort of way,

and say, "Does it?"

As We Turn onto Rose's Street

Luke glances over at me and starts
drumming on the wheel with his fingertips.
Then he clears his throat and says,
"Do your parents know about this?"

"About what?" I say,
pretending I don't get what he means.
"About that lad being there tonight," he says.
"Oh," I say. "Sure. But they trust me."

And it's true.
They do.
Because they know
that Taylor's gay, too.

As Taylor's fond of saying,
he's never even set *foot* in the closet.
Except to kiss Matt Hopkins that one time
when they were in sixth grade.

So yeah.
Everyone knows
that Tay's gay.
Except for Luke, I guess.

When We Pull Up in Front of Rose's House

Luke switches off the motor.
Then he turns to me,
looking very serious, and asks,
"Will this girl's parents be home tonight?"

"Geez," I answer.
"For someone who doesn't have any kids,
you're excellent at this interrogation stuff."
"Will they be home?" he asks again.

"Sure," I say. But I say it like I'm *not* sure.
All of a sudden, Luke reaches out
and puts his hand on my knee.
On my *knee*.

He looks at me for a long moment.
Then he gives it a little squeeze
and says, "Well, just don't . . .
Just don't do anything you'll regret."

"Oh, I won't," I say, as casual as anything.

Then I Thank Him for the Ride

And as I hop out of the car
and head up Rose's front walk,

I can feel his eyes
following me.

Or
can I?

Last time I thought he was watching me,
it turned out he was watching his phone.

So I glance back over my shoulder,
just to check,

and see that this time,
he's looking at *me*.

Looking right *at* me
with this real weird expression on his face.

Almost like he's jealous.

I Ring the Bell

The door swings open,
and Taylor and Rose pull me
into a bone-crushing hug.

"It's Triatomic time!" Taylor shouts,
as we chase each other up the stairs
to Rose's room.

And while we munch on popcorn,
Rose launches into a story about
this guy she met in Cape Cod named Vic.

She tells us he's incredibly cute,
and that he pretended he was drowning
just so she'd swim out and save him.

"Which is exactly what I did," she says.
And then she smiles this dreamy smile
and doesn't utter another word.

"Nooooo . . . ," Taylor and I moan in unison.
"You can't stop there," he says.
"Yeah," I say. "It's a need-to-know situation."

Rose laughs.
"It's not nice to kiss and tell," she says.
Then a second later she adds,

"But I'm not that nice."

So She Tells Us

That when they got back to shore,
she said, "You didn't need to pretend to drown
to make me notice you. I already had."
And when he asked how she knew he was faking,
she said, "I was watching you out there, dude.
You're an amazing swimmer."

Then she closes her eyes and sighs.
"Turns out he's also an amazing kisser.
And amazing at . . . everything else."
"*Everything* else?" I gasp.
"Has our Rose been deflowered?" Taylor cries.
"Deflowered?" she laughs. "Lord no."

Then she tells us
it was just a lust thing, not love.
So she didn't let him get past second base.
"I would've dumped him if he'd pushed for more,"
she says. "I'm saving the rest for Mr. Right.
Though we did do a lot of dry humping."

"And God," she adds,
"if just doing *that* feels so good,
can you imagine how great
having actual sex must feel?"
"I don't have to imagine it," Taylor says.
"I found *out* how it feels."

And Rose and I both shriek.

Taylor Laughs

And says, "Don't get so excited.
There's nothing much to tell."
But then he proceeds to tells us
"nothing much" for the next half hour—

all about how when he first noticed Evan
sitting alone in the chem lab,
and Evan looked up from his experiment
and spotted him,

there was this
overwhelming feeling
of this-is-it-ness
between them.

Then he tells us
that the strangest part is
that Evan isn't even
that good-looking.

"But," Taylor says with a faraway look in his eyes,
"we have the most amazing chemistry . . ."
Then he snaps out of it and adds,
"Pun intended."

And we all crack up.

But When We Ask Him About Going All the Way

He says, "That part's private.
Though it did involve some private parts."
Rose groans and says,

"We respect your decision not to tell us."
"But we hate your decision," I add.
Then we both say how happy we are for him.

And he says it'll happen to us someday, too.
"But how will we know for sure
that we've found the right guy?" Rose asks.

He thinks this over, then replies,
"Well, it's probably different for everyone.
But for me, it was when I realized

that it wasn't just my body talking—
it was my mind and my heart, too.
And they were all saying just one word."

"One word?" I ask, my voice almost a whisper.
"Just one word . . . ," Taylor replies.
"And that word was 'Yes.'"

Then we all leap up and start dancing
around the room, chanting, "Yes! Yes! Yes!"
until we dissolve into a fit of giggles.

When We Finally Stop Laughing

And we're just lying here on Rose's bed,
catching our breath, she turns to him and says,
"You did use protection, though. Right?"
"Of course we did," he says.
"We're way too young to be dads."
And we all crack up again.

Then Taylor asks me
if *I* fell for anyone this summer.
I nibble on my lower lip.
I've never mentioned Luke to them.
I didn't meet them till he was already in Kenya,
so there was never any reason to.

I wonder what they'd think if I told them
about him right now—and if I told them his age.
"I kind of have a crush on an older guy," I say.
"Oooo . . . ," Rose says. "How old?"
"Old enough to drive?" Taylor asks.
"Yeah . . . ," I say.

"Old enough to vote?" Rose asks.
"Yeah . . . ," I say again.
"Dude," Taylor says, grabbing his heart.
"Please don't tell us he's old enough to drink."
So I don't. I just tell them it doesn't matter anyhow,
because the guy doesn't feel the same way about me.

And then—I change the subject.

I'm Trying to Fall Asleep

But I can't.
And it's not just because
Taylor and Rose seem to be having
some kind of snoring contest.

It's because
I can't stop thinking
about what happened with Luke
earlier tonight.

I can't stop flashing
on how warm his hand felt
when he rested it
on my knee.

I can't
stop reliving
that little squeeze
he gave it.

To Luke,
it was probably no big deal.
Just an innocent little
knee squeeze.

But
to me—
it felt like
the opposite of innocent.

The Next Morning

We're making blueberry pancakes
while discussing what to wear
to the first day of ninth grade,
when Mom texts to say Luke's picking me up.

And he'll be here in ten minutes!
Taylor offers me the first pancake,
but suddenly I'm not hungry.
I swipe on some lip gloss and try to tame my curls.

Then I sit here, pretending to act interested
in the conversation, while I wait . . . and wait . . .
and wait . . . Until finally, after the longest
half hour in history, a horn honks.

I say goodbye, and dash outside.
As I hop into Luke's car, he says, "Sorry I'm late.
I got hung up looking at an apartment."
"Oh . . . ," I say. "That's okay."

And he must have seen my face fall
at the thought of him moving out,
because he gives me a little wink and says,
"Don't worry. I hated the place."

I laugh, as a flash flood of relief washes over me.
Then he says, "Your parents are off to a wedding today,
so Alice talked me into taking you two to the beach."
Oh my *God*. I love my little sister.

At the Beach

Luke leads us
past all the noisy families,
past the teens flinging Frisbees,
and the couples snuggling on blankets,

leads us
past the tide pools,
across some big rocks,
and around a bend.

And there,
stretched out before us,
is a totally deserted strand of sand.
"Our own private beach!" Alice cries.

Then we're spreading out our blanket,
and stripping down to our bathing suits,
and I'm trying not to stare
at Luke's bare chest,

trying not to blush
as his eyes drift across my skin,
warming every inch of me
like he's my own personal sun.

And Then Alice Is Tugging Us Toward the Water

And we're crashing into the icy surf,
splashing each other and screaming,
and diving and ducking and catching waves,
and Luke's sneaking up behind me and tickling
my ribs and I'm shrieking and tickling him back

and Alice is squeaking, pretending she's a dolphin,
and then Luke's a shark, and Alice and I are mermaids,
and now Luke's pouncing on me and we're laughing
wildly and going under, swirling together
in a frothy tangle of arms and legs.

And a few seconds later, when we bob back up
to the surface, we're suddenly face to face.
And he smells like coconut and cocoa,
and we're just standing here
gazing into each other's eyes . . .

And then—
Alice is a sea horse, splashing us
with a vengeance, whinnying and giggling.
And that's when we notice that her lips are blue
and her teeth are chattering.

So Luke lifts her onto his shoulders
and takes hold of my hand.
(My hand!)
Then together we walk back
to our blanket on the sand.

Now the Air Feels Icier Than the Water

My teeth start chattering.
Luke notices right away,
and wraps me in a towel.

I catch sight
of the scar on his arm,
and shudder.

What if that leopard
had done more
than just bite him?

Luke pulls Alice into his lap,
and hugs her
till she stops shaking.

He settles her on a corner of the blanket,
with a juice box and a bag of chips.
Then he smiles at me and says, "Your turn."

He sits down next to me,
puts his arms around me,
and holds me close.

"Just relax, luv," he says. "Breathe."
But there's no way I can possibly do
either of those things right now.

In Fact

If anything,
my shivering seems
to be getting worse.

We sit here like this for a few minutes,
while the sky fades from blue to violet
to pink to gold . . .

And after a while, we become aware
of the sound of Alice's steady breathing.
We look over and see that she's asleep.

"We've tuckered the poor lass out,"
Luke says. "We better let her doze awhile."
Then he holds me even closer.

But my shivering just won't stop.
Is it because of the breeze
that's blowing in off the water?

Or because Luke has his arms around me?

We Watch the Waves Rolling In and In and In

And then finally,
the heat from Luke's body fills me up
and my shivering stops.

"There," he says, brushing a damp curl
off my forehead. "That's much better."
But he doesn't stop holding me close.

He glances
up and down the shore.
"Our own private beach . . . ," he murmurs.

Suddenly
he's cupping my face
in the palms of his hands,

looking into my eyes
like he's searching for an answer,
our faces only inches apart.

And now he's kissing my lashes . . .
my cheeks . . . my chin . . .
Now he's leaning in

and gently pressing his lips to mine.

Whoa . . .

Then Suddenly—It's Over

I open my eyes,
and for a split second
I wonder if I imagined the whole thing.

But when I see how he's looking at me,
how his dark eyes are gleaming,
I know it really happened.

"I'm sorry," he whispers.
"I shouldn't have done that."
"Oh yes you should have," I say.

And then we grin at each other.
And I feel so . . .
so *connected* to him—

like we're these two
ridiculously happy people
sharing one madly beating heart.

But

Just as he leans in
for a second kiss,

we hear
Alice yawning,

and we have to wrench
ourselves apart

and act like
nothing has happened—

like the course of both our lives
has not just been

changed forever.

I'm Lying Here in Bed

Staring up at the glow-in-the-dark stars
on my ceiling—the ones Luke gave me,
back when I was Alice's age.

I'm lying here remembering
how we stood on my bed that night
as I told him where to stick each one.

How when he was finished,
we lay down side by side
and Luke switched off the light.

How he took hold of my hand
as we watched the stars glow to life
for the very first time . . .

I'm lying here,
in that same bed right now,
remembering how magical it was.

And tonight,
as I let my fingers float across
the stones on my necklace,

remembering the thrill that ran through me
when Luke pressed his lips to mine,
I feel like *I'm* glowing to life.

I feel like I'm made of magic.

The Next Day Is Labor Day

And Rose texts me,
begging me to come over
to save her from her relatives.

But I tell her I've got
my own relatives to contend with.
We're throwing a big family barbecue.

Dad's firing up the grill.
Mom and Luke are chopping veggies
for the salad.

And I'm shucking corn with Alice,
the two of us giggling
as we fold the husks halfway down—

turning the ears
into little yellow ballerina dolls
wearing corn-silk tutus.

I'm sneaking peeks at Luke.
But he's so busy goofing around with Mom
he docsn't even notice me.

Though when she asks me to bring
the folding chairs up from the cellar,
he volunteers to help me.

Suddenly every atom in my body is on high alert.

He Opens the Cellar Door

And when
he rests his palm
on the small of my back
to guide me down
into the dark,

it feels
like a spark
igniting a flame
that's singeing me
right through my tee.

When We Get to the Bottom Step

I reach for the light switch.
But Luke covers it with his hand.

Then he turns me around
to face him,

tips my head back,
and leans in to kiss me.

Only he doesn't kiss me.
He just bring his lips close to mine—

so close
I can feel him breathing.

"Are you sure about this?" he whispers.
"Positive," I whisper back.

Then he finally
lets his lips touch mine,

and his kiss ripples
all through me,

like perfect circles
on the surface of a secret pond.

Each Time

We climb back up the stairs
with another two chairs,

I'm a little
more flushed,

a little
more hushed,

a little
more dazed,

a little
more crazed,

a little
more *more*

than the time
before.

Then Uncle Mike and Aunt Pat Arrive

And we spend the afternoon playing ping-pong
and badminton and H-O-R-S-E with all our cousins,
while gorging on hot dogs and corn and s'mores.

As the party winds down, my cousin Heather
tries to teach me how to do the splits.
But I'm hopeless at it.

I glance over and notice
that Luke's watching me,
grinning at my lame efforts.

He winks at me and starts gathering up
a pile of used paper plates.
"I'll just toss these in the bin," he says.

As he heads down the driveway
and disappears behind the garage,
I tell Heather I'll be right back.

Then I grab some crumpled napkins
and empty soda cans, and follow after him.
Behind me, I hear Mom laughing with my aunt.

"Looks like our Lilybelle has a little crush on Luke,"
Mom says. "Isn't that adorable?"
And as I slip behind the garage, I'm thinking,

Not as "adorable" as it seems, Mom.

I'm Lying in Bed

With one hand on my necklace,
the other pressed to Luke's wall,
the first time I hear them:
three quiet little taps.

They're so faint,
I think maybe I've imagined them.
But then they come again:
Tap. Tap. Tap.

I hesitate for a second,
then tap the wall three times.
Luke answers right away
with three more taps.

A little zing
shoots up my spine.
We're sending messages
in a secret code!

Me: *Tap. Tap. Tap.*
Luke: *Tap. Tap. Tap.*
Me: *Tap. Tap. Tap.*
Luke: *Tap. Tap. Tap.*

I don't know
what Luke's three taps mean.
But I know what mine mean:
I. Love. You.

The First Day of High School

Isn't nearly
as scary as I thought
it would be.

Probably because
my cousin Heather filled me in
on all the important stuff.

She's in college now,
but she went to the same
high school.

So she told me how to find the cafeteria,
and what's too gross to eat
(everything).

She told me where all the bathrooms are,
and which ones to stay out of
(all of them).

What she didn't tell me
is how I'm going to survive
being away from Luke,

all day long,
five days a week,
week after week after week.

But Then I Walk into French Class

And there's Taylor and Rose,
grinning at me and waving,

shouting, "*Bonjour, Mademoiselle Liliette!*"
as they pat the empty seat between them.

This is how
I am going to survive.

When I sit down, Taylor studies my face
and says, "You look . . . different."

"Yeah," Rose says. "It's weird.
Like you're glowing or something."

Oh my God—are Luke's kisses
written all over my face?

I swallow hard and say, "We were
at the beach this weekend. I got a tan."

"No . . . ," Taylor says.
"It's more than a tan . . ."

But then the bell rings—
and I'm saved by it.

In Creative Writing Class

Mr. Bennett said we all had to write a concrete poem—
a poem whose shape is as meaningful as its words.
So I wrote this:

Luke and Lily,   Lily and Luke,
Luke and Lily, Lily   and Luke, Luke an
d Lily, Lily and Luke,   Luke and Lily, Lily and
Luke, Luke and Lily, Lily and Luke, Luke and
Lily, Lily and Luke, Luke and Lily, Lily and
Luke, Luke and Lily, Lily and Luke, Luke
and Lily, Lily and Luke, Luke and Lil
y, Lily and Luke, Luke and Lily, Lil
y and Luke, Luke and Lily, Li
ly and Luke, Luke and Lil
y, Lily and Luke, Luke
and Lily, Lily an
d Luke, Luke
and Lily
Lily a
nd
L

But I'm not going to turn it in.

I'm Plowing Through the Multitudes

Trying to get to geometry before the bell,
when I glance down the hall and notice Jason,
that guy who kissed me after the dance last year,
heading in my direction.

Suddenly
I'm a little nauseous—
remembering how it felt when he poked
his slimy tongue into my mouth.

Jason's eyes meet mine for a second.
Then both of us look away.
And as he passes by,
our shoulders almost touch.

I shrink away from him,
thinking back to that awful night
when I told myself that there had to be
more to kissing than that.

And I can't help smiling to myself.
Because now I know I was right—
there's whole worlds more to it.
Whole galaxies.

At Lunch with the Triatomics in the Quad

Rose is devouring my chips, telling us
about this guy, Presley, in her math class.
"He's not my type," she says.
"But I think *you* might like him, Lil."

"Wait a minute," Taylor says. "Back up.
Since when do you have a type?"
Rose pops a chip into her mouth and says,
"I've developed a thing for redheads."

"What color is Presley's hair?" he asks.
"Blond," she says, "with a little streak of blue."
"Darn," I say. "I've developed a thing
for guys with brown hair."

Taylor narrows his eyes at me.
"Does your 'older guy' have brown hair?"
"Is that why you look so glowy?" Rose says.
"I told you," I mumble. "It's a tan."

"Good," Taylor says. "Then why not
let Rose introduce you to Presley?"
"Because . . . ," I say.
"His name is too annoying."

"Well," Rose says, "when you see him,
you might change your mind."
But I just shrug, and think to myself,
Not gonna happen.

Photography Class

As the students filter into the room,
Mr. Lewis meanders between our desks,
snapping pictures of us and asking us our names.

His long dreadlocks, his goatee,
and his purple high-tops officially make him
the coolest-looking teacher ever.

Just before the bell rings, a guy dashes in
and hands a slip to him—he's cute,
but not in an I-know-I'm-cute kind of way.

Mr. Lewis snaps a picture of him
and says, "Welcome, Presley.
Take a seat right over there next to Lily."

Whoa . . . This is the guy we were just talking about.
I can't help noticing his walk—so relaxed and
confident, like how a cowboy might walk.

He eases down onto his chair,
wipes his too-long bangs out of his eyes,
and flashes me a smile.

Rose was right. I might have been
interested in someone like Presley.
If I weren't already in love

with someone like Luke.

In Chemistry

Some wiseass asks Ms. Peyser
why we should be interested.
She tells him that chemistry helps us
understand the world around us.

That everything you can smell
or touch or taste is a chemical.
That fireworks
are based on chemistry.

Taylor nudges me and whispers,
"All this talk about touching and tasting
and fireworks. It's making me miss Evan."
I smile at him and roll my eyes.

But I know
exactly how he feels.
And I wish I could *tell* him that—
tell him all about Luke and me.

Though he almost had a heart attack
at the thought of me dating
someone old enough
to drink.

If I told him
I've been kissing
a twenty-nine-year-old man,
what would he think?

After School

Taylor dashes off to FaceTime with Evan.
Our moms won't be picking us up till four,
so Rose and I head straight
to Bella's Bookshop.

The sign in the window says:
50% USED. 50% NEW. 100% AWESOME.
And it really is—I mean, there's even
a special section just called "LOVE."

I don't have a godmother.
But if I did,
I'd want her to be exactly like Bella—
funny, wise, and totally un-judgey.

Plus, she's got this exotic fortune-teller vibe.
She wears all these rings and colorful scarves,
and long skirts with tiny tinkly bells
sewn right into the fabric.

Once,
she even closed up shop a little early
so she could give us a belly dancing lesson.
(She called it Bella dancing.)

But the thing we like best about her
is that she seems to know things about us.
Deep things. Sometimes even before we do.
Bella is 100% awesome.

I Tug Open the Heavy Oak Door

And take
a whiff of that comforting
dust-and-books-and-cookies smell.
"Darlings!" Bella cries, her big red smile
turning her face into a wild party.
"How I've missed my two love-story addicts."

She hugs me, then pulls back to study my face.
"Look at you," she says. "You're positively radiant.
Are you in love? Or merely pregnant?"
"Only if the Lord knocked her up," Rose says,
giving me a nudge. "Or some *other* older man."
Bella narrows her eyes at me.

"Don't worry," I say. "It's an unrequited crush."
My ears burn. I've never lied to her before.
I get the feeling she senses something's up.
But she doesn't press me, she just raises an eyebrow,
then turns to hug Rose and says,
"What about you? Any unrequited crushes?"

"Nope," Rose says. "Mine was requited."
"Hmmm," Bella says, "I can see that . . . But this guy . . .
He wasn't Mr. Right. He was Mr. Right Now."
"God, Bella," Rose says. "How do you *do* that?"
"It's a gift," she says with a shrug. "My granny cast
a spell over me the day I was born. I guess it took."

And I'm pretty sure she's dead serious.

Bella Goes Behind the Cash Register

Then she slides a stack
of love stories across the counter,
beaming like she wrote them herself.
"These arrived last week," she says.
"But I didn't even put them on the shelf.
I was saving them for you two."

"*Wuthering Heights*! *Rebecca*!" Rose cries.
"A signed copy of *The Fault in Our Stars*!"
"These are amazing," I say. "*You're* amazing."
"I am, aren't I?" Bella says with a grin.
"And when your love affair with love ends,
I'll turn you kids on to Beat poetry."

"Oh, it'll never end," I say.
"Love stories like these
keep our hearts pounding."
"Yeah," Rose sighs, clutching
If I Stay to her chest. "Nothing even *close*
to this romantic will ever happen to us."

All of a sudden, I'm biting my lip,
fighting an overwhelming urge
to tell them that my life *is* a love story.
Better than a love story, even.
And then the door swings open—
and in walks Luke!

When the Guy

Who you've been trying
not to tell your friends about

suddenly shows up
in the very same room with them,

and walks straight over to you,
right in front of them,

saying, "There you are, Lily.
Your mom told me I'd find you here,"

you have to command your face
not to give you away,

you have to
take a deep breath,

you have to turn to your friends,
as calm as anything,

and say, "This is Luke.
He's a friend of the family."

And you have to say this
like that's *all* he is.

You'd Think Rose Would Realize

That Luke is my "older guy."
You'd think Bella,
with all her intuition and stuff,
would pick up on us right away.

But Luke's flashing his smile,
turning it on like the beam from a lighthouse.
And now he's hypnotizing them
with that devastating English accent of his.

He's asking Bella
if she chose that blouse
because it matches her eyes,
or if it's just a happy accident.

He's telling Rose
he's heard she fancies love stories,
asking her to tell him what it is about them
that intrigues her so.

In other words,
they're both way too busy
having their pants charmed off
to see what's staring them right in the face.

Finally

Luke buys me *Rebecca*,
then blinds Bella and Rose
with one last smile,
and whisks me out the door.

A few minutes later, we're sitting in his car
on the rooftop level of the parking lot
at the mall where no one really goes anymore.
Luke switches off the motor.

Then he lays out what he calls the "ground rules."
I don't really like the idea of him giving me rules.
He's acting like he's my dad or something.
But I guess they make sense.

He says we can't call each other on the phone.
Someone might overhear us.
He says we can't send emails or texts either.
Someone might read them.

And handwritten notes
are out of the question.
"How about telepathy?" I ask.
"Is telepathy okay?"

He laughs and says, "Absolutely not."
"Then how will we communicate?" I ask.
"Here's how," he says.
And he leans in for a kiss.

But Then My Phone Rings

And it's Mom,
checking to make sure
Luke picked me up.

She says she's sorry
she couldn't be there herself,
but they're hanging a new show at the gallery.

She says she'll have to work till six all week.
But Wanda's mom has agreed to take Alice
home after school with her every day.

And she says Luke is such a sweetheart,
he's offered to pick *me* up.
Every afternoon for a whole week!

Then she asks how my first day went.
She asks if Taylor and Rose
are in any of my classes.

She asks if we can buy
some basil on our way home.
And I answer all her questions.

But it's hard to keep
the quiver out of my voice.
Because the whole time we're talking,

Luke is kissing the nape of my neck.

As We Circle Around and Around

Heading back down to the ground level
of the parking lot, and to reality,
Luke says he can hardly wait till I turn eighteen.

"On your eighteenth birthday,
I'll put up billboards all over town
and take out a full-page ad in the newspaper.

On your eighteenth birthday,
I'll hire one of those planes
with a banner streaming behind it.

On your eighteenth birthday,
when it's finally legal for us to be together,
I'll tell the whole world about us."

Then, just before we pull out into the street,
he reaches over, takes my hand, and says,
"Can you promise to keep us a secret till then?"

I want to tell him yes, yes I can.
But I just smile and nod.
Because I'm way too dazzled to speak.

A Few Minutes Later

When we stop off at the market
to get the basil for Mom,

Luke buys a bouquet of white lilies
for her too.

But when we get back into the car,
he hands them to me,

saying,
"Lilies for my Lily."

And my heart
blooms in my chest.

But Then

Just before we get home,
he says that even though they're for me,
we'll have to pretend they're for my mom.

All of a sudden,
I've got a giant lump in my throat.
I feel ridiculously close to tears.

"*We'll* know, though," Luke says,
with a reassuring smile.
"You and I will know they're yours."

When we walk into the kitchen,
he whips the bouquet out from behind his back,
and presents it to Mom with a deep bow.

"These are for you, Julia," he says.
"For being so gracious about
letting me camp out here for so long."

She gives him a playful shove.
Then she takes the flowers,
my flowers, and says,

"Don't be silly.
You've been such a help with the kids.
Honestly. We need you here, Luke."

And she pulls him in for a hug.

They Are My Flowers

But Mom
gets to choose the vase.

Mom gets to
arrange them.

I want to put them
on my dresser,

where I can feast my eyes on them
while I fall asleep.

But Mom sets the vase
on the kitchen table.

They are
my flowers.

Mine.

It's the Middle of the Night

I've been lying in bed
for hours,

rubbing the stones on my necklace
as if each one is a tiny genie lamp . . .

I can't take it anymore.
I just can't.

I throw back the covers
and slip out of my room.

I tiptoe to Luke's door
and press my cheek to the cool wood.

I can feel him
yearning for me—

yearning for me right now
on the other side of this door.

I suck in a breath
and take hold

of the gleaming glass knob.

But I Don't Turn It

I pull
my hand away,

slink down the stairs,
and hurry to the kitchen.

I reach
for one of the lilies,

tear off some petals,
and sneak back up to my room.

Then I climb into bed,
open *Rebecca*,

and press the petals
in its pages.

Except for one—
the one that I tuck underneath

my pillow.

In Creative Writing

We're supposed to be working
on in-class essays about
what we did during summer vacation.
Stunningly original topic, right?

Mr. Bennett wrote on the board
that we had to include at least two similes,
and that we should remember
to "show" instead of "tell."

Then
he set a timer
for thirty minutes.
That was around ten minutes ago.

I'm glad he didn't say
how long our essays had to be.
Because I'm already finished with mine,
and it's pretty short:

*This summer, I felt like a wish that had finally
been fulfilled. I felt like a dream that had
finally been remembered. But I can't tell you
why, because you told us not to "tell."*

*And I can't "show" you why either, because
that would be telling. The other kind of telling.
And I promised someone I wouldn't.
The End (and also The Beginning)*

Photography Class

Mr. Lewis wanders
through the room with his camera,
pausing now and then to snap a picture
of one of us, as he talks about portraits.

He says when we photograph
another human being,
we learn something about
what makes them human.

He says our cameras can see things
we can't see with our naked eyes.
"When a portrait is done well," he says,
"it reveals secrets about its subject."

Then Mr. L turns and snaps *my* picture.
"Ack!" I cry, covering my face with my hands.
"Don't worry," he chuckles. "I'll never tell."
And the whole class cracks up.

I sneak a peek at Presley.
He's laughing along with everyone else.
But he's got the kindest look on his face,
like, *I feel you, girl.*

So I smile my thanks, and start laughing too.
Even though I'm sort of worried . . . I mean,
what did my portrait reveal? What did Mr. L see?
Did he see all my secrets? Did he see Luke and me?

In Madame Melvoin's Class

I know I'm supposed
to be thinking about
French verbs.

But all
I can think about is
French kissing.

And about
Luke's lips pressing
against mine.

All I can think about
is the fact that ten minutes from now,
when the bell rings and I rush outside,

mon amour will be waiting for me.

I Hop into Luke's Car

And I'm just about to beg him
to take me somewhere, anywhere,
so we can kiss, when—

"Surprise!" Alice shouts,
popping up like a jack-in-the-box
from the backseat.

I let out
a startled shriek
and she giggles wildly.

She says, "Wanda's throat got strepped,
and the nurse sent her home.
So Mom asked Luke to pick me up.

And he's gonna buy us books at Bella's!
Isn't he the most wonderfulest man in the world?"
"Yes," I say. "He is."

And Luke and I
exchange a very quick,
very frustrated glance.

But Then I Realize

That if Bella sees Luke and me together again,
she might sense that something's up.
So I claim I've got too much homework.

He smiles at me and says,
"No worries, luv. We'll make it snappy."
And his English accent just about undoes me.

A few minutes later, we're walking into Bella's
and she's welcoming us with a platter
of her homemade peanut butter cookies.

Luke takes a bite and says it's positively brilliant.
And Bella's just about undone, too.
She blushes deeply and thanks him.

Then Alice says, "We're making it snappy, luv!"
And starts tugging Bella to the children's section,
asking her to show her the ballerina books.

Luke puts his hand on my shoulder,
and this little thrill shoots through me
as he guides me toward the "LOVE" section.

I glance back at Bella and catch her watching us.
For a split second, I see this look in her eyes—
this look like she *knows*.

But then she blinks, and it disappears.

On Thursday After School

When I hop
into Luke's car,

Alice shouts "Surprise!" again,
and starts giggling her head off.

I whirl around and shoot her a look
that's less than friendly.

I love Alice,
but it wasn't even funny the first time.

Apparently,
Wanda is still home sick.

Someone had better get that kid
some stronger antibiotics.

Right *now*.

Thursday Night

I'm lying
on my bed,

under the twinkling Milky Way
of my glow-in-the-dark stars,

having my nightly tap fest
with Luke.

Tap. Tap. Tap.
Tap. Tap. Tap.

And I'm thinking
how ridiculously amazing it is

that he actually
waited for me.

That he waited for me
to grow up.

Just like
he promised me he would.

Friday After School

Alice pops up
out of the backseat
again.

Like an instant replay
of the afternoon before.
Only worse.

Because now
it's been three whole days
since Luke and I have kissed.

Or held hands.
Or had a single second
alone together.

My
whole body aches
with wanting.

I wonder—
can a person
actually die of desire?

I Didn't Realize Luke Overheard Me Yesterday

When I was telling Mom
how amazing Mr. Lewis is.
And how even though he said it's okay
to use my old point-and-shoot for assignments,
I can't help wishing I had a better camera.

I didn't realize that Luke heard Mom apologizing,
telling me we can't afford to buy one right now.
And that he heard me trying to make her feel better,
telling her that actually, I kind of like
the challenge of using the one I have.

I didn't realize
Luke heard any of that.
But he must have—because just now,
when Mom and I were doing the dishes,
he walked in and gave me a fancy new Nikon.

And even though Mom was right there,
I flung my arms around him.
But she just smiled fondly at me,
like she thinks my "crush" on Luke
is the cutest thing ever.

It's So Strange

To be at this party
with Taylor and Rose tonight,

so strange to be
laughing and joking

and snapping all these pictures of everyone
with my brand-new camera,

so strange to be playing
this game of truth or dare,

and to have to keep on
taking the dares

because I can't risk
having to tell anyone the truth.

Which is that I don't
actually want to be here.

And that I'd give anything
to be out on a date right now instead—

out on a date
with the boyfriend

that no one even knows I have.

And Then, to Make Matters Worse—

Presley shows up.
And Rose brings him right over
to introduce us.

He smiles at me, swipes his bangs out of his eyes,
and says, "Oh, we've already met. We're in
photography together. Isn't Mr. L cool?"

I answer that yes, Mr. L is totally cool.
And Presley says that he likes what he told us
about how our cameras can see things we can't see.

And while we're talking, I steal a glance at Rose.
She's smirking at me with one eyebrow raised,
silently mouthing, "I can see things too."

Just then, Taylor walks up,
and Rose asks him and Presley
if they'd mind scoring us some nachos.

As soon as they head off, she turns to face me.
She crosses her arms over her chest,
but doesn't say a word.

"Okay. Okay," I say. "I didn't tell you we'd met
because *this*—I knew you'd make a big deal out of it.
Presley's great. But we're just friends."

"Sure you are," she says with an I-told-you-so grin.

On Saturday Morning

When I come downstairs for breakfast,
Mom's helping Alice into her jacket.
"I've got a sore throat, too, now,"
Alice croaks cheerfully. "Just like Wanda!"

Mom says she's taking her
to Dr. Gold to see if it's strep.
She says, "Dad's out buying doughnuts.
He'll be back in five minutes."

My heart begins pounding.
As soon as the front door
swings shut behind them,
I dash upstairs to my room.

I go straight to the window
and peek through the curtain,
trying to calm the flock of butterflies
that's just flitted into my stomach.

I watch as Mom bundles Alice into the car.
Then, the second they drive away,
I race to my door, yank it open—
and there's Luke,

standing right in front of me
with this huge grin on his face.
He says he's sorry Alice isn't feeling well.
But not *that* sorry.

He Gathers Me into His Arms

And kisses me with such force
that our teeth crash together.

He's breathing hard,
pressing his hips against mine.

And when I feel the effect
I'm having on him,

it's like I've morphed
into Super Lily or something—

like there's this strange new power
coursing through my veins . . .

Then We Hear a Car

Dad!

Luke wrenches his lips away,
and grips me by my upper arms,
his dark eyes drilling into mine.

"What are you doing tonight?"
he whispers urgently.
"I'm . . . I'm sleeping over at Rose's," I say.

He leans in
for one more kiss—
a kiss so passionate it almost hurts.

Then he pulls back and murmurs,
"I know a beautiful spot . . . A spot
where we could kiss like this all night."

And somehow, by the time
Dad walks through the front door,
Luke and I have come up with a plan.

He gives me one more fierce kiss,
then heads downstairs,
as calm as anything,

while I waft into my room,
and ease the door shut behind me,
my whole body vibrating.

Geometry's Usually So Easy for Me

But when you've just arranged
a secret rendezvous,

it's impossible to focus
on your homework,

to concentrate on acute angles
instead of on your soul mate's *cute* ones,

to think about anything except
how incredibly much you love him,

and about the fact
that if all goes as planned tonight,

the two of you will finally be able
to be alone for hours,

and your only chaperone
will be the man in the moon . . .

I let my fingers glide
over the smooth green stones

of the necklace I never take off,
and drift into a delicious daydream . . .

Then—*Wham!*

My bedroom door flies open.
Alice zooms in and starts
bouncing up and down on my bed.
"Haven't you ever heard of knocking?" I growl.
Alice stops bouncing.

Her lower lip trembles.
She looks so flushed and feverish.
"I'm sorry, Lilybelle," she rasps.
"But knocking takes too long.
And I needed to tell you the big news."

She flops down next to me, swiping at a tear.
Now I feel like a total jerk.
"Aw, that's okay," I say. "You'll understand
about privacy when you're older."
I hug her and ask her to tell me her news.

"I've been strepped!" she rasps.
"Just like Wanda!"
She looks deliriously happy about this.
Or maybe just delirious.
"Wow," I say. "You're twins!"

And after Mom feeds her some chicken soup,
Alice and I snuggle on the couch, acting out
"ballets" with the animals Luke gave her.
All except for the leopard—
which Alice claims she lost.

After the Animals Take Their Final Bows

Alice rests her head on my shoulder
and falls asleep.

That's when I become aware
of the conversation in the kitchen.

Luke's telling Dad that he's going out
with Amber again tonight.

"I've got a feeling I might get lucky," he says.
"So don't worry if I don't come home."

Suddenly,
it's a little hard for me to breathe.

Because Luke's not really
spending the night with Amber.

But *telling* my dad that he is,
is step #1 of our plan.

And when I think about who he might
actually be spending the night with,

it gets even harder
to breathe.

Because It Just Dawned on Me

That when Luke and I
came up with our plan,

we didn't have time
to talk about what we'd do.

He did mention
kissing all night.

But what if he's expecting
to do more than that?

What if he thinks
I'm more experienced than I am?

(i.e.:
not at all.)

I feel a little dizzy—
like I might faint or something.

Man.
I have got to get a grip.

What I Pack in My Overnight Bag:

My toothbrush,
my toothpaste, my new camera,
my reddest lipstick,

and my clingy green dress,
the one that matches
my tsavorite necklace.

Then I tuck in my laciest bra.
Then I take it back out.
Then I shove it back in.

Then I yank it back out again.
Will Luke see me in this tonight?
Am I ready to go to second base?

I have no clue.
But I stuff the bra back into the bag,
slip in my copy of *Rebecca*,

and zip it up
before I can change
my mind.

When Mom Drops Me Off at Rose's

I walk
in the door,
and get right to the point.

"Will you guys be my alibis tonight?" I say.
They exchange a quick glance,
then squeal with delight.

"Do our ears deceive us?" Taylor gasps.
"Are you actually gonna do something naughty
for once in your life?"

"Oh my *God*," Rose says. "It's Presley, isn't it?"
"Tell all," Taylor says. "Immediately.
It's a need-to-know situation."

So I swallow hard and then explain
that it isn't Presley, it's the older guy I've been
crushing on—he's finally asked me out.

"Exactly how old is this guy?" Taylor says.
"Old enough to have a midlife crisis?" Rose says.
"Old enough to wear adult diapers?" Taylor says.

And then they both crack up.
"Ha. Ha," I say, rolling my eyes.
"Seriously, though," Taylor says.

"How old *is* he?"

The Question Hangs in the Air Like Smoke

I wish
I could just tell them the truth.
But they'd go bonkers if they knew
how old Luke really is.

"Um . . . Not that old," I say.
"He's . . . He's only twenty-four."
"Whoa . . . ," Rose says. "He's almost
twice your age. That dude's messed up."

"I don't think that's even legal," Taylor says,
bugging out his eyes at me.
"He must be some kind of freak," Rose says.
"He's not a freak," I protest. "He's amazing."

But they just fold their arms
over their chests,
and refuse to cover for me.
They say it's for my own good.

They say anyone that old
who wants to date someone my age
must have some serious issues.
"What are you guys?" I ask. "My parents?"

"No," Rose says, putting her hand on my arm.
"We're your best friends. Who love you."
"And who'd never forgive ourselves," Taylor adds,
"if you ended up in a ditch somewhere."

I Feel Like Screaming at Them

And telling them they're being idiots.
But I will myself to stay calm.

"Come on, guys," I say.
"He's not a serial killer. He's just . . . older."

"He's not just 'older,'" Taylor says.
"He's practically a pedophile."

"Yeah," Rose says.
"The guy's a perv."

It's obvious I'm not gonna
be able to change their minds.

So I sigh and say,
"I guess you're right."

Even though they're as far from right
as anyone has ever been

in the entire history
of the universe.

Luke is not a perv.
He's not like that at all.

I Wait Just Long Enough

So that it won't
seem suspicious.

Then I tell them I have to pee,
and head upstairs to the bathroom.

I pull apart
the curtains,

and flash the lights
on and off three times.

And a few seconds later,
when I look down the block

and watch Luke's car
drive away,

a little piece of my heart
goes with it.

I Don't Want to Be Here

I'd call my parents
and ask them to come and get me,
if I could handle all Mom's questions.

Or the fact that Dad
wouldn't even bother
to *ask* me any.

I'm so pissed at Taylor and Rose
for ruining what might have been
the best night ever.

Though I mean, a part of me gets it—
they only refused to cover for me
because they care about me.

So I don't want them to feel guilty.
Which is why I try not to mope around,
acting like my life is over.

But it takes
just about every speck
of strength I have.

Because I seriously doubt
that anyone on earth has ever felt
more like their life is over

than I do right now.

It's Exhausting

Fending off all of my friends'
prying questions about Luke,

exhausting listening to them go on and on
about why dating him is such an awful idea,

exhausting pretending to be okay,
when I am the opposite of okay.

So it's a huge relief when they
finally nod off.

I grab my backpack
and reach for *Rebecca*,

desperate to escape my own reality
and lose myself in Mrs. de Winter's.

But then I see my lacy bra,
balled up in the bottom of the bag,

right next to the beautiful camera
that Luke gave me.

And suddenly I miss him so much,
it feels like my chest is cracking in two.

In the Morning

The sun streams in
through a gap in the curtains
and warms me awake.

For a few minutes,
I just lie here,
floating in the golden glow of it . . .

But then I remember—
I remember what *didn't*
happen last night.

I run my fingers over
the stones on my necklace,
a river of tears rising in me.

Ugh. I don't want Taylor and Rose
to see me crying . . . But when I glance around
the room, I realize they aren't here.

And just then,
they burst in with a plateful of bacon
and hold it right under my nose.

"Even people dating pervs gotta eat," Taylor says.
"Yeah," Rose says with a sympathetic smile.
So I force a smile of my own

and manage to choke down a strip.

Then

While Rose finishes
the last few pages of *Wuthering Heights*,
I shoot some portraits of Taylor.

He keeps striking all these goofy poses,
in a not-so-subtle attempt to cheer me up.
So I do my best to pretend it's working.

But I get so into trying to capture
how the sun lights up his eyes,
that after a while I really *do* get cheered up.

A few minutes later,
Rose slams her book shut,
and clutches it to her chest.

"*Gah*," she says. "Catherine never
should have wasted all those years on Edgar
when she was so in love with Heathcliff."

"Let me guess," Taylor says.
"Heathcliff was . . . a redhead?"
Rose flings the book at him.

"I'm fresh out of love stories," she says,
tugging me up off her bed.
"Let's go to Bella's."

But By the Time We Get There

My sadness is back, weighing me down
like a jacket made of lead.

I slip on my I'm-totally-fine-
you-don't-have-to-worry-about-*me* mask.

But Bella isn't fooled.
She takes one look at me,

rests her palms on my shoulders,
and says, "This too shall pass, my darling."

Then she reaches behind the counter
and hands me a book.

It's hard not to start sobbing
when I see the title: *Love Finds a Way*.

She wraps her arms around me
and strokes my hair.

"It *does*," she murmurs.
"If it's meant to be."

Funny word—"if."
So tiny, but so enormous.

Before We Leave

I ask Bella if I can take her picture.
She balances a stack of books on her head
and grins at me.

I snap a bunch of different shots,
until I've captured it all—her humor,
her sparkle, and her kindness.

Then she lifts the books off her head.
"I'll be right here," she says,
"when you're ready to talk about it."

And as we head out of the shop,
I realize there's a lump
the size of a lemon in my throat.

Taylor and Rose each take hold
of one of my hands and walk me down
the block to the ice cream shop.

But it's not until I take
my first bite of rocky road
that I notice my throat feels even rockier.

Oh no . . .
This isn't a lump in my throat.
I've been strepped.

I Text Mom to Tell Her I'm Sick

And fifteen minutes later,
when Dad comes to pick me up,

I'm starting to feel
like I've been hit by a truck.

I've got chills, my whole body aches,
and there's a brush fire raging in my throat.

I wish Dad could lift me up
and carry me to the car.

But I'm not
a little girl anymore.

And he hardly ever picked me up,
even when I *was*.

When we get home and walk in the door,
there's Luke—

snuggling on the couch with Alice,
reading her the Sunday comics.

He looks up, and our eyes lock.
Just long enough

for our secrets to pass between us.

Alice Leaps Up

And dashes over to me,
with Luke right behind her.

She hugs me and says, "I'm sorry
I strepped you. But now *we're* twins too!"

"That's okay," I say,
patting her tangled curls.

"Our poor lovely Lily," Luke says.
"So sorry you're under the weather."

He's looking at me like he wishes
he could hug me too.

Like there's so many things
he'd be saying to me right now,

so many things
he'd be *doing* to me right now,

if only
we were alone.

(Which would probably really turn me on
if I weren't feeling like the walking dead.)

When Your Mother

Won't stop brewing you cups
of chamomile tea

and taking your temperature
and plumping up your pillows,

right when you want to feel
more grown up

than you
ever have before,

it makes you feel
like screaming.

Only you can't.
Because your throat hurts too much.

After a Nap, I'm Feeling a Little Better

Well enough to go downstairs and watch
Alice in Wonderland with my sister.
Well enough to hope that Luke
will come and sit by me on the couch.
And he *does*. Almost instantly.

He snuggles down
under the blanket with Alice and me,
then secretly presses his thigh to mine.
If I didn't have a fever already,
this definitely would've given me one.

But a second later, Mom comes in
from the kitchen and shoos him away.
"Better not sit so close to Lily," she says.
"She'll be contagious till tomorrow
when the antibiotics kick in."

"Excellent point, Julia," he says.
Then he gets up,
letting his hand brush
against my knee for a split second,
before he moves over to the rocking chair.

When I Wake Up on Monday

My throat feels like it's lined with gravel.
I take a sip of orange juice
and wince at the sting.

Dad pats my head,
tells me to rest up,
and dashes off to work.

Alice has been cleared to go to school.
"Feel better soon," she says,
blowing me a kiss.

"It's lucky you're such
a great student, Lilybelle," Mom says.
"Missing one day of classes won't hurt you."

She gives me a quick hug,
and thanks Luke for volunteering
to take care of me while she's at the gallery.

"Please don't find an apartment anytime soon,"
she calls as she hurries Alice out the door.
"I don't know what I'd do without you, Luke."

And as soon as they drive away,
he's behind me—
wrapping his arms around me.

He Nuzzles the Nape of my Neck

And says, "You weren't faking, were you?
So we could be alone together?
Please tell me you were faking."

"That would've been genius," I croak,
as I lean back against him.
"But it really does hurt."

"Well," he says,
letting his lips brush my ear,
"then I guess we shouldn't kiss.

But there are
other things
we can do.

We can't let
this stroke of good fortune
slip through our fingers."

It's hard to think
of feeling this crappy
as a stroke of good fortune.

But I know
he didn't mean it
like that.

When Luke Said

That there were
other things we could do,

I knew he was talking about more
than just holding each other close.

I figured he meant
going to second base.

And now, as he takes me by the hand
and leads me off,

I'm ready
for that to happen.

I'm ready to let
the man I love touch me

where no one
has ever touched me before.

Luke Steers Me Toward the Living Room

I hesitate in the doorway,
my stomach clenching—

all the walls in there
are covered with family photos,

Mom and Dad smiling at me
from every single one of them.

"Um . . . I think I'd rather
go to your room," I rasp.

But he just laughs and says getting
caught in bed together would be a disaster.

He says you never know when someone
might come home unexpectedly.

"Besides," he adds, "we'll be much more
comfy on the couch than in my tiny bed."

Then he scoops me into his arms
and carries me over the threshold

like I'm his bride.

As We Cross the Room

Heading
toward
the couch,

I realize
that I'm holding
my breath.

Mom and Dad's eyes
are following me
from every picture frame,

their
smiles
fading . . .

And with each step Luke takes,
the distance between the doorway
and the destination seems to

widen—
like this is all
just a strange dream . . .

Then Somehow—We're There

And he's lowering me
onto the cushions.

So gently,
as if I'm made of glass.

And now he's darting
from window to window,

closing
the curtains.

The room's getting darker,
but there's still enough light

for me to see
those family photos.

For me to see
my parents staring at me.

Luke sits down next to me,
and murmurs,

"Alone at last."

He Looks into My Eyes

He tells me
how beautiful I am.
How perfect.

He starts
kissing my neck,
then kissing my shoulder,

then kissing
his way down
my arm,

kissing
and kissing and kissing
till he reaches my hand.

Then he spreads open my palm,
pressing his lips into the center of it.
It's so romantic, I can hardly stand it.

And now,
it's not just my throat
that's on fire.

But All of a Sudden

Luke stops kissing my palm
and presses my hand down onto his knee.

He sucks in
a sharp breath.

Then he takes hold of my wrist
and begins guiding my fingers,

guiding them
   up along his thigh,

      guiding them
         so slowly. . .

            up . . . and up . . .
               and up . . .

                  toward . . .
                     toward . . .

His Crotch!

Wait . . .
What?

This isn't
what was supposed to happen.

He hasn't even
touched my breasts yet.

Not even
the outside of my T-shirt.

I've listened to enough
of Rose's descriptions

of what she did (and didn't do)
with the guys she's dated

to know
that some major steps

are being skipped right over.

And That's When I Remember

I remember what Taylor
told Rose and me about Evan.

How he knew it was right because
his body and his mind and his heart

were all saying
just one word.

And I realize that my body
is saying, "I'm not ready for this."

My mind is saying, "Not here,
with my parents watching."

And my heart?
My heart doesn't know *what* to say.

I Try to Pull Away

But Luke just tightens his grip
on my wrist

and starts murmuring
about how long he's waited,

how long he's waited
for me to touch him like this,

and about how the kissing's been lovely,
the kissing's been brilliant,

but a man needs more,
more than kissing,

and he'll go mad,
stark raving mad

if we don't take things
to the next level.

Then suddenly—
he reaches down with his free hand

and with
one smooth motion,

he unzips his fly.

But

Just as he's about
to press my hand down
onto his boxers,

I hear
myself saying, "Stop!"
in this weird strangled voice.

And that's when
I finally manage to wrench
my wrist free.

Luke lets out this awful groan.
I shrink away from him,
pulling my knees up to my chest.

He rakes his fingers through his hair.
"I don't get it," he says.
"I thought you cared about me.

I thought you wanted to make me feel good.
I thought you were a woman.
But maybe you're still

just a kid."

His Words Burn

Like a slap across the face.
"I'm not a kid, Luke. I'm *not*."

"Then please, Lily. Touch me.
Touch me like a woman touches a man."

I look into his dark eyes
and realize there's tears in them.

Tears.
I can't stand it.

I can't stand
making Luke this unhappy.

I squeeze my eyes closed,
so I can't see my parents watching.

Then I grit my teeth
and let him ease my hand onto him,

fighting back tears
of my own.

He Moans

And whispers the words I've waited
all my life to hear him say:

"I love you, Lily.
I love you . . . I love you . . ."

My heart feels like
it's going to burst.

"I love you too, Luke.
I love you so much."

But I don't understand
how a person

can feel so awesome
and so awful

at the exact same time.

He Sighs

Like he's never
felt anything so good in his life.

Then suddenly he gasps,
and scrunches up his face,

almost like he's in agony
or something.

A second later,
his head drops back against the couch,

and I realize
he's finished.

As he sits there with his eyes closed,
catching his breath,

I get this weird feeling—
like he's forgotten I'm even here.

And a couple of minutes after that,
his mouth falls open, and he starts snoring.

I turn away from him and curl up
into a ball on the cushion beside him.

The Next Morning in Photography

Mr. Lewis wanders around the room,
snapping photos of our hands.
"Our hands are full of stories," he says.
"Stories about what they've made,
what they've held, what they've touched . . ."

My cheeks blaze as I flash on what mine
were touching just yesterday.
"Our hands are our autobiographies,"
he says. "Show me a man's hands
and I'll show you his passions."

"Oooo . . . ," some loser behind me snickers.
"I'd rather see a *woman's* passions."
Mr. Lewis whirls around to face him.
Then he gives the kid the finger!
The class sits here in stunned silence.

"You see?" Mr. L says. "My hand told him
the whole story with one simple gesture."
And we all crack up.
Then he asks us to study the hands of the person
sitting next to us, to see what we can learn.

Presley and I exchange a glance.
I have to fight the urge to sit on mine,
to keep him from seeing them.
Because I mean, what if, you know,
it shows?

But Then

I tell myself
to stop being ridiculous.

And when
Presley says, "You first,"

I put one thumb in each of my ears
and waggle my fingers at him.

"Hmmm," he says, stroking his chin.
"I see you've had a very . . . a very *silly* life."

I cross my eyes and he laughs.
So I laugh too.

And
I'm not sure why,

but joking around with Presley,
with a boy my own age—

makes me feel like a bird
that's been freed from its cage.

At Lunch with the Triatomics

Taylor says he and Evan are brainstorming
ways to use chemistry to stop global warming.
He says they still can't believe Trump
pulled out of the Paris Climate Accord.

He says Trump's sure got a lot of nerve.
Then Rose points out
that "nerve" rhymes with "perv."
And Taylor asks if I'm still seeing *mine*.

This sort of thing
happens all the time lately.
They always manage to work
the conversation around to Luke.

They won't stop grilling me,
and giving me these penetrating looks,
like they're trying to see into
the very depths of my being.

Though I've gotten
so good at rolling my eyes,
so good at laughing off
their endless questions,

so good
at convincing them
their imaginations are working overtime,
that sometimes *I* even believe me.

Luke Isn't Able to Get Me Alone Again

Till Wednesday, when Mom goes to the dentist.
He picks Alice and me up from school,
then drops her off at ballet.

"We better hurry," he says,
giving my knee a quick squeeze.
"Her class will be over in forty-five minutes."

He steps on the gas, pushing every red light,
till we're back at the deserted
rooftop parking lot at the mall.

He ushers me into the backseat with him,
kisses me for a while, then unzips his pants
and asks me to do the same thing I did last time.

When I reach for him, he moans,
then locks his hands behind his head
and starts telling me he loves me.

But I can't figure out
why I feel so . . . so . . . Oh, I don't know.
Sort of lonely, I guess.

I mean, he's saying he loves me.
But does he love *me*?
Or what I'm *doing* to him?

Love Is Strange

Stranger
than it is
in books.

Not anything
like it is
in books.

Not to Mention Confusing

I mean,
I should feel happy
that Luke wants to be alone with me so often.
Shouldn't I?

So how come when he picked me up
after school today and told me we could
sneak off to the parking lot for an hour,
I felt the opposite of happy?

When we got there,
he tugged me into the backseat,
unzipped his fly, and asked me to do
the same thing as the last two times.

But even though he said he loved me,
being with him didn't seem
as romantic as it used to be—
back when all we were doing was kissing.

And his kisses felt . . . different today.
He pressed so hard it was like
he was trying to pulverize my lips
with his.

So hard I wanted to pull away
and say, "You're hurting me!"
But he might have thought
I was acting like a kid if I did that.

On Sunday

Dad finally decides to take some time off.
So the whole family, plus Luke,
spends the morning together.

We rake up the oak leaves in the front yard
into an enormous pile.
Then we all leap into it—even Dad.

Luke throws a handful of leaves at me,
and then everyone's throwing leaves
at everyone else,

and we're laughing and shouting
and leaves are fluttering down all around us
like pieces of golden confetti.

And for once, Luke doesn't even try
to shoot me any secret glances.
But I don't miss them one bit.

The truth is,
it feels great to just
be having fun with him—

to just relax and not have to deal
with that constant tightness in my chest,
that constant pressure I feel

whenever Luke and I are alone.

Which Luke Thinks Isn't Nearly Often Enough

We've been
meeting in secret
for a couple of weeks now.

Last week, he only managed
to take me to the parking lot twice.
Which was two times more than I wanted to go.

But today when we went, there was
caution tape stretched across the entrance.
And a sign saying the mall is officially closed.

Luke banged his hands
on the steering wheel
and cursed.

I heaved a secret sigh of relief.
"Guess we'll have to improvise," he said,
more to himself than to me.

Then he drove us down
the dirt road that winds into the woods
behind the 7-Eleven.

And for some reason,
doing it to him there made me feel
even lonelier than usual.

Now That the Mall Is Closed

It seems like all week long
when I'm at school and Luke's
supposedly out looking for apartments,

or writing up his research
for the foundation
that sent him to Kenya,

he's really just driving around,
scouring the city for places where we can
"have our privacy," as he refers to it.

I refer to it
as places where he can
"get me to do it to him."

God.
I can't believe I just said that.
I sound so cynical.

I don't think
I like the person
I'm becoming.

In Photography

Today Mr. Lewis says
he wants us to take portraits of each other.
Then he pops his camera into my hands.
and asks me to study him through the lens.
I swing it up to my eye and take a look.

"What do you see?" he asks.
"I mean, besides my beautiful brown skin?"
The class laughs.
"Well," I say. "I see . . . I see the light
from the window reflected in your eyes."

"Excellent observation," he says.
"And today, while you're shooting your portraits,
I want all of you to focus on the eyes.
The eyes aren't just the *windows* to the soul.
The eyes *are* the soul."

Then he begins pairing students up
and sending them out the door with their cameras.
"Don't just look," he calls after them. "See!
Let *your* eyes see the secrets in theirs."
And then—

Presley asks Mr. L if *we* can be partners.

As Soon as We Get Outside

He turns to me and says,
"I promise not to let you see *my* secrets,
if you promise not to let me see *yours*."
"Deal," I say. And we both laugh.

Then I admit that I hate
having my picture taken.
"My smile always feels so fake," I say.
"like it's been taped onto my face."

And Presley says
he feels the same way.
And I'm not really sure whose idea it is
to do what we do next.

But we find
an old *People* magazine on a bench,
and start leafing through it
for smiles.

Then
we tear them out,
hold them up in front of our mouths,
and snap portraits of each other.

I wiggle my eyebrows and Presley starts laughing,
letting his paper smile fall from his face.
And that's when I snap a picture of his real one.
And I can't help thinking how nice it is.

And When the Bell Rings

And Presley asks me for my number,
so we can send each other
our favorite shots later,
I don't think anything of it . . .

Now, it's almost midnight.
And I've been lying on my bed,
looking at the pictures we took
of each other.

We both look so . . .
so relaxed . . .
so happy . . .
so *young* . . .

And when my phone buzzes and it's Presley,
texting to ask if I want to check out the new
photo exhibit at the museum on Saturday,
I text back **Yes!** without even thinking.

Because it'll just be two friends,
with a common interest, hanging out.
It's not a date or anything.
I mean, it's not like I'll be cheating on Luke.

Then I hear three taps on my wall,
and my tsavorite necklace
somehow seems to grow a little tighter
around my throat.

Saturday Morning

When Mom asks me
if I can babysit for Alice today,
I tell her I'm sorry but I can't.

When she asks me why,
I tell her I'm meeting someone
at the museum.

When she asks me who I'm meeting,
Luke strolls into the room
and Presley's name freezes in my mouth.

"Oh . . . ," I say. "Just a friend
from photography class."
"A new friend?" Mom says. "That's nice."

"Yeah," I say. "We're gonna
check out the Diane Arbus exhibit."
"Well," Mom says. "I'm sure you girls will love it."

"Um . . . Yeah," I say. "It's supposed to be great."
But I can feel Luke's eyes on me,
feel them drilling into me,

searching for my lie.

Saturday Afternoon

Presley and I
are at the museum,
wandering through
the galleries.

"These portraits are awesome," he whispers.
"They totally reveal their subjects' secrets."
"Yeah," I whisper back.
"Just like Mr. L said."

We move on to a picture of twin little girls,
staring right at us with big creepy eyes.
"Whoa," Presley whispers.
"I don't think I want to know *their* secrets."

And we're laughing quietly at this,
our shoulders almost touching,
when I happen to glance toward the door—
and see Luke!

He's not even looking in our direction.
But somehow I know he's seen me.
Seen that I'm here with Presley, not with a girl.
His face grows pale, while mine flames up.

There may not be a portrait of *me*
hanging in this gallery,
but my secret has definitely
been revealed.

A Few Seconds Later

When I sneak a peek
in Luke's direction—he's gone.
And so is my carefree mood.

I don't
see him again
until a few hours later.

I'm in the front hall,
waiting for Mom to find her always-lost keys
so she can drive me to Rose's for a sleepover.

I'm passing the time
snapping photos of Alice, who's doing
another one of her "goodbye ballets" for me.

Suddenly,
Luke walks in the front door,
holding hands with a woman.

Picture
the most beautiful actress
you can think of.

This woman
is ten times more beautiful
than that.

A billion times more beautiful than me.

Luke Grins at Us

"Oh, hey," he says, as casual as anything.
"Julia, Alice, Lily—this is Amber.
Amber, meet my three favorite girls."
Mom looks as stunned as I am.

"I thought *I* was your favorite," Amber says,
giggling at her own dumb joke.
"It's . . . It's lovely to meet you," Mom says.
"Oh, you too, Julia," Amber coos.

She reaches out to pat Alice on the head.
But she scowls and ducks out of reach.
"Aren't you a shy little thing?" Amber says.
"No," Alice says. "I'm not."

Amber ignores her remark and turns to me.
"And you must be the wannabe
photographer Luke mentioned.
You're just as cute as he said."

"Isn't she, though?" Luke says.
Then he leads her right past us and up the stairs,
murmuring, "Let me show you that thing
I was telling you about."

"I'm off to my sleepover, Alice,"
I say in a voice that's almost a shout.
"I'll tell Rose and *Taylor* hello for you."
And Luke almost trips on the stairs.

160

Rose Swings Open Her Door

And says, "Oh, Lil. We're *so* relieved."
"You're finally over your perv!" Taylor cries.
"Over my . . . perv?" I say.

"Oh come on," Rose says.
"We know you and Presley are a thing.
He told me all about your museum date."

"So," Taylor says,
"give us some juicy details.
It's a need-to-know situation."

And suddenly I realize
that if they think I'm with Presley
they'll stop bugging me about Luke.

So I force
a smirk onto my face,
and tell them Presley and I had fun.

Then I make a gesture like I'm zipping my lips.
Taylor grins and says I am a very wicked girl.
And I say he is absolutely right.

Then Rose Gets a Text and Almost Faints

It's from Quinn,
a sophomore she met yesterday.
He's throwing a party tonight
and wants us to come.

Rose says
he's got the most beautiful red hair.
She says she thinks
he might actually be "the one."

And I'm happy for her.
Really. I am.
But I'm so not in the mood
to go to a party.

I don't have any choice, though—
since I'm even less in the mood to go home
and listen to Luke and Amber doing
God knows what through my bedroom wall.

Which doesn't even make any sense.
Because I don't even *like* doing that stuff to him.
So why does the thought
of *her* doing it to him

make me feel like I can't breathe?

Rose's Brother Drives Us Over

We step through Quinn's front door.
It's sweaty in here—the kind of sweaty
that happens when there's too many people
jammed into way too small a space.
The music's blaring, the bass so heavy
I can feel each beat in the soles of my feet.

"I'm gonna go find Quinn," Rose shouts,
her eyes bright as she heads into the crowd.
It parts like a curtain, then swallows her up.
"Text Presley," Taylor calls over his shoulder,
as he starts dancing with a guy in a top hat.
"Tell him to meet you here."

But the only person I feel like texting is Luke.
Suddenly, images of him and that woman,
and of what they're probably doing
right this very minute,
start churning through my mind
like poisonous fumes.

Then a girl pops a beer into my hand.
I tried beer once. I hated it.
But that doesn't stop me
from chugging this one.
Or the next one.
Or the next . . .

And Pretty Soon

I'm dancing
and laughing and dancing
and bumping into all the other dancers
and they're bumping into me
till we're just one big
tangled dancing mass
and I'm spinning in circles,
spinning all thoughts of Luke
right out of my head,
whirling and swirling and twirling
and getting so dizzy I have to stop
and flop down onto the couch
and then there's a guy sitting next to me
and his arm's around my shoulder
and his grin's too wide for his face
and he's telling me he's been watching me
and that I'm a great dancer
and then he's leaning in
like he's about to kiss me
and his breath smells like something
much stronger than beer . . .
And that smell . . .
That smell . . .
It's like a match
lighting the fuse on a bomb.
And that bomb is my stomach.
And then—I'm leaping off the couch
and puking my guts out.

Sunday Morning

So *this*
is what a hangover feels like.

I shade my eyes
from the daggers of sunlight

stabbing into the room
through the gap in the curtains,

and run my tongue
over my parched lips.

"Girl," Taylor says,
"what came over you last night?"

"Yeah," Rose says.
"Since when do you drink?"

Their words detonate in my ears.
I groan and clamp my hands over them.

"Please," I beg. "Not so loud."
"Sorry," they whisper in unison.

And even *that* hurts my head.

Rose Gets Some Toast and Advil into Me

Then she and Taylor drag me over to Bella's.
By the time we get there,
I'm only feeling really awful.
Which is a big improvement.

Bella raises an eyebrow when she sees me.
Then she smiles sympathetically and says,
"Each new experience teaches us
what we *do* and do *not* want to do."

"I'll say," I mutter, as she wraps me in her arms.
I inhale her dust-and-books-and-cookies smell.
Then she pulls back to take a closer look at me.
And when Taylor and Rose wander out of earshot,

Bella says, "So tell me, my darling.
Which hurts more—your head or your heart?"
I think about Luke and Amber
and my eyes fill with tears.

"I guess it's sort of a tie," I say.
Bella gives my hand a little squeeze,
then leads me over to the self-help section.
"Browse," she says.

But
I don't need
self-help books—
I just need Luke.

How He Treats Me Now

Like nothing
ever happened between us.

Like we never kissed or touched
or said I love you.

Like I'm not a day older
than Alice.

How That Makes Me Feel

Like a bug
that's been splattered
on a windshield.

Every Single Night

Luke goes out.
And I lie here on my bed,
staring up at the glow-in-the-dark stars,

my fingers drifting across
the smooth green stones
on my necklace.

I try to fall asleep,
but I can't stop thinking about Amber.
About her blue eyes gazing into Luke's.

About her lips on his.
About her hands touching him
the way mine used to.

All of it's so awful,
like a love song gone wrong,
making every hour that passes

feel
a million
minutes
long.

And School Is No Better

In French, we conjugate *souffrir*:
You suffer. He suffers. I suffer.
Vous souffrez. Il souffre. Je souffre.

*Je souffre
et je souffre
et je souffre.*

At lunch, Taylor and Rose
ask me why I'm so miserable.
I just shrug and say,

"I'm a teenager. I'm allowed to be moody."
"Point well taken," says Taylor.
But neither of them looks any less worried.

In creative writing, I work on micro fiction:
*She loved him. She lived for him. He left her.
She lived on. But she was dead.*

In geometry, we study parallel lines.
But I sit in class,
dreaming of a parallel universe—

a universe
in which Luke and I
are still together.

And Presley's Been a Problem Too

Lately, he seems to be everywhere at once.
It's like there's multiple Presleys roaming around.
I'm constantly bumping into them.

And he won't stop smiling at me
and shoving his adorable too-long bangs
out of his eyes.

It's like having a puppy you're allergic to—
you really want to pat him,
but you know it wouldn't be a good idea.

I wish he'd quit acting
like our trip to the museum
was our first date or something.

Because it really wasn't supposed to be.
And a second ago, when I finally worked up
the courage to tell him I just wanna be friends,

I could actually see
the light leave his eyes.
Like I'd switched off a lamp.

Now, I'm just standing here watching him—
realizing that he *looks* exactly like I *feel*.
And knowing that I've made him feel like that?

Well it's making me feel even worse.

Then

After seven endless days—
there's a miracle.

I'm sitting at the kitchen table
when it happens.

Mom's at the sink peeling carrots.
I'm staring at my chemistry book,

trying to make sense of the words
as they swim across the page like minnows.

But I'm distracted by Luke's gentle voice,
reading to Alice in the next room.

It fills me with such longing,
my chest feels like it's splitting apart.

I groan and put my head down on the table.
Mom asks me what's the matter.

And when I tell her I hate my life,
and that I especially hate chemistry,

Luke saunters into the room
and offers to tutor me.

Just like that.

The Next Day, He's Waiting for Me After School

My heart swells as I hop into his car
and we zoom away.
He glances over at me and smiles.
I smile back.

"Ready for our first tutoring session?" he says.
"Uh-huh," I manage to croak.
He doesn't say anything else.
So I don't either.

But as I sit here, watching his hands
guiding the steering wheel,
I notice the scar the leopard left on his arm
and a shiver races through me.

I want to tell him
how much I've missed him.
I want to tell him that Presley's just a friend.
And that Taylor is too.

I want to tell him
how hideous it's been
picturing him with Amber every night.
But that'd make me sound

like a lovesick little teenager.

He Drives Us Over to the Research Library

It's at the university where he got his doctorate.
He takes me into a private study room
with a big glass door.

There's no lock on the door,
but there *is* a venetian blind.
Luke tugs it closed.

Then he sits down on a wooden chair
and motions for me
to take the seat next to his.

Suddenly everything
I've been trying so hard not to say
comes gushing out of me.

And then
he's telling me
that he missed me too

and that Amber meant nothing to him
and that he only started seeing her
to make me feel jealous.

"Well, it worked," I say.
And then we're both laughing,
and he's covering my lips

with his.

He's Kissing Me

Kissing me
so softly, so sweetly,

just like he used to,
way back in the beginning.

"When you were a kid," he whispers.
"I promised I'd wait for you."

Then he kisses me again and says,
"You were so worth the wait."

And it's lucky we're not outside,
or I'd float right up out of my seat

into the sky.

When We Finally Come Up for Air

I ask, in my flirtiest voice,
"Aren't you supposed to be tutoring me?"

"There *is* an awful lot
I want to teach you," he says.

And as he unzips his fly,
a smile spreads across his face—

a smile that somehow reminds me
of the Big Bad Wolf.

"But today," he says, taking hold of my hand,
"we'll just review what you already know."

And as he presses my fingers
down onto him,

this weird combination
of relief and revulsion washes over me.

I haven't lost him to Amber after all.
He's still mine.

And if this is what it takes
to keep him,

then this is what I'll do.

When It's Over

He zips up his fly
and puts his arm around my shoulder.

"So," he says. "You hate chemistry?"
"Not anymore," I say.

He laughs and says, "Seriously, though.
Are you passing? Flunking? What?"

So I tell him the truth—
that I'm actually doing fine.

That I've got a B+ average
in the class.

That I was just in a rotten mood yesterday
when I was complaining to my mom.

"Well," he says, "then I guess
you'll have to start getting some Ds.

And then, very slowly,
work your way up toward Cs."

I Shudder and Bite My Lower Lip

Because when you've worked hard
and done well in school all your life,

it's not easy to wrap your head around
trying to get Ds.

But when I tell Luke that messing up
in chemistry will ruin my grade point average,

when I tell him I want to go to college,
a *good* college,

he just pats me on my head
and tells me not to worry.

When I say I don't like the idea
of flunking tests on purpose,

he laughs and says we'll bring
my grade back up by the end of the year.

When I ask him if he's sure about that,
he doesn't answer.

He just leans in and kisses me.

I'm Sitting Here in Chemistry

Taking a quiz
on vapor pressure and liquids

and how they reach
their boiling point,

feeling like
I'm about to reach *mine*.

I know
every single answer,

but Luke told me to get
at least a third of them wrong.

He said if I do too well,
there won't be any reason

for him to keep on
"tutoring" me.

Though this pretending-to-be-dumb thing,
I didn't know it would make me feel

like I've got the starring role
in a very bad play.

At Lunch

Rose asks Taylor and me
how we did on our chemistry quiz.

I mumble something about
boiling points being my downfall.

"But that quiz was easy," Taylor says.
"And since when do you have a downfall?"

"Yeah," Rose says. "You are, and always
have been, a downfall-free zone."

She's right.
I always have been.

But am I anymore?

A Few Days Later

Luke's waiting after school again,
to drive me to the library
for our second weekly "tutoring" session.

We go up
to the same study room as before
and he pulls the blinds closed.

He starts kissing me right away.
But they're those crushing kind of kisses.
Not the romantic kind.

He backs me up against the wall,
and grinds his body against mine
till it feels like I'm getting black and blue.

"I've been trying to take it slow," he whispers.
"Trying so hard . . . But I'm not sure
I can go on like this much longer."

"I'm not sure I can either," I say.
And as he eases me down onto the chair
next to his, and unzips his fly,

he's completely unaware
that *my* words
mean the opposite

of his.

He Presses My Hand Down onto Him

An eternity passes.
Then, just after Luke finally finishes
and zips his fly back up,

the door
to the study room
springs open!

A guy says, "Whoops. Sorry.
Didn't know anyone was in here."
"No problem, mate," Luke says with a smile.

But as soon as the door closes,
it slips from his face.
"That was a bloody close call," he says.

And suddenly I'm shaking.
I'm shaking and I can't stop.
"We shouldn't come here anymore," I say.

"Don't worry, Lily. I'm working on
finding a better place for us. And until then,
we'll just have to be a little more careful."

"A *little* more careful?" I say.
"Okay," he says with a chuckle.
"A lot more careful."

On the Way Home

I stare out the window of the car
and notice pumpkins

grinning at me from front porches
all over the neighborhood.

Their burning eyes
remind me of Luke's.

It's hard to believe
Halloween is only two weeks away.

They say time flies
when you're having fun.

But I guess it flies
just as fast

when you're having no fun
at all.

On Saturday, I Go to a Sleepover

And even though I'm sitting right here
in the same room with Taylor and Rose,
I feel like I'm on
an entirely different planet.

Because when Rose starts talking
about her all-consuming crush on Quinn,
and Taylor starts gushing about Evan
and about how much he misses him,

I can't really chime in and tell them
about my "tutoring" sessions with Luke.
If they knew how old Luke really was
and what we were doing, they'd freak.

And they don't make it any easier
when they bring up the topic of Presley.
Which of course they *do*, since talking about
him seems to be their new favorite hobby.

Rose says she knows why
I told him I only want to be friends.
And Taylor says it's obvious
that I'm still sneaking off with my "perv."

I deny it—but they don't believe me.

The Next Morning

When we go to Bella's,
she says she needs my help in the back room.

Which is just a way to get me alone
so she can ask me personal questions.

Like: "So how's your love life been lately?"
I tell her it's nonexistent.

But she sees through me
as easily as if I'm made of Saran Wrap.

I can tell
by the look on her face.

Though she doesn't
say anything.

She just offers me an oatmeal cookie,
the tiny bells in her skirt tinkling.

And for some reason,
the sound of them makes me feel

like crying.

At Lunch with the Triatomics

I'm listening to Rose talking about
how excited she is that Quinn asked her
to the Halloween dance.

And about how
they've already begun working
on their Beauty and the Beast costumes.

I'm listening to Taylor swooning
about how thrilled he is that Evan's
coming to town for the festivities,

and about how he can't wait for us to meet him,
and about how they're planning to go to the dance
dressed as Chicken and Waffles.

I'm listening
to both of them going on and on and on
and suddenly I find myself wishing

I was going to the dance with Presley,
dressing up as a camera and a tripod
or whatever—

wishing that my life
was as simple and uncomplicated
as theirs.

At Our Third "Tutoring" Session

Luke tugs down the venetian blind.
Then he pushes his chair
right up against the door.

"I'm still looking for a better place," he says.
"But in the meantime, at least no one
will be able to barge in on us."

Even so,
the whole time I'm touching him,
my blood's pounding in my ears.

Then, when he finally finishes, my phone buzzes.
It's a text from Rose, with a photo attached.
She's modeling a poufy yellow prom gown.

Below it she's written: 1st try at my Beauty
costume for the dance. Thoughts?
Luke glances at my screen.

"Your school's having a Halloween dance?" he asks.
"Why?" I sigh. "Are you gonna ask me to go?
Like a real couple?"

"How I wish I could," he says.
"Though we *are* a real couple, Lily."
"Yeah," I say. "A real couple

who can't even be seen in public together."

Luke Pulls Me onto His Lap

He says he wishes things were different.
He wishes we could go on dates.
He wishes he could take me to the dance.

Then he pauses, like he's thinking.
And a second later, his face lights up—
like he's gotten the best idea ever.

"You know what?" he says. "You should go.
Go to the dance with Taylor and Rose."
"I . . . I should?" I say.

"Absolutely. Just because
we can't celebrate Halloween together,
that doesn't mean *you* shouldn't be able to."

I can feel
my pulse quicken.
"Are you sure you wouldn't mind?" I say.

"Of course not," he says, kissing my cheek.
"Just put on a clever costume and go out
and have a brilliant time with your mates."

And
I'm so excited,
I hardly even mind

when he unzips his fly again . . .

It's Hard to Come Up with a Costume

When you aren't
half of a couple.

I obsess over it for a few days,
bouncing ideas off the Triatomics.

But in the end,
I just give up

and decide to go
as Little Red Riding Hood—

because Taylor has an old red cape
with a hood attached that I can borrow,

and Rose has
a nice little red skirt.

Besides, I know a thing or two
about how to handle the Big Bad Wolf.

Way more than
I'd *like* to know.

Before the Dance

We all meet up at Rose's house.
And even though Evan is dressed as a waffle,
I can see right away why Taylor likes him.

Because when we're introduced, he gets this
real serious look on his face, and asks me what
I'm bringing to Grandma's house in my basket.

He says he sure hopes
it isn't chicken. Or waffles.
And we all crack up.

I can see why Rose likes Quinn, too.
His Beast costume shows off his broad shoulders.
He looks like he walked straight out of a love story.

And the way he beams at her—
you can see how much he admires her.
And not only because she's pretty.

Both couples seem . . .
Well, they just seem
so meant-for-each-other.

I used to think Luke and I
were meant-for-each-other too.
But lately,

I'm not so sure.

Rose's Brother Drops Us Off at School

We weave through the throngs of trick-or-treaters
on the sidewalk, and head into the dance.
It's amazing what a bunch of pumpkins
and gauze and plastic skeletons can do for a gym.

And with the fluorescent lights
turned off like this, and just a bunch
of tiny orange bulbs twinkling everywhere,
you could almost say it has atmosphere.

I'm dancing with Taylor and Evan and Rose
and Quinn, only feeling a tiny bit sorry for myself
that I don't have an actual date—
when Presley shows up!

He's dressed as a woodcutter.
I shoot Rose a look, but she tries (and fails)
to act like she has nothing to do
with this astonishing "coincidence."

Presley doesn't say anything.
He just grins,
slings his cardboard ax over his shoulder,
and starts dancing with me.

He's got great moves—
cool, but kind of goofy at the same time.
Like he's poking fun at his own dancing skills.
It's . . . It's ridiculously adorable.

After a Half Hour

Of the best time
I've had in forever,
the DJ starts playing a slow song.

Rose rests her head
on Quinn's shoulder.
Taylor holds Evan tight.

Presley and I watch, as both couples
close their eyes and begin to sway,
drifting off into the crowd.

Then he turns and looks at me,
like, *Do you want to?*
And I tell him with my eyes that I do.

He smiles and holds out his arms.
But just as I'm about to slip into them,
a dark shadow looms up from behind him

and this guy wearing a wolf mask
steps right in front of him,
slips his hands inside my cape,

wraps his fingers around my waist,
and before I even have a chance to protest,
he dances me

away.

I Glance Back Over My Shoulder

And see
Presley's face,

see the shock
and disappointment.

His shoulders sag
as he turns and walks off.

I've got to go after him!
I struggle to break free.

But the hands around my waist
just tighten their hold.

And the menacing gleam in Luke's eyes
seems to paralyze me.

Here We Are

Finally out in public together.
As close as we've ever gotten
to being on a real date.

And because Luke's wearing a mask,
and the lights are down so low,
he can hold me as close as he wants.

There was a time
I'd have given anything to be out
with him like this, dancing in his arms.

Though now that it's actually happening,
his arms feel like tentacles,
squeezing the life out of me.

"It was almost too easy to sneak in here,"
he whispers. "I just went round back
and told them I was helping out the DJ."

He grabs my hips under my cape
and grinds up against me, murmuring,
"I knew you'd love this surprise."

But I don't love it.
I don't love it
at all.

As the Song Nears Its Finish

Luke's holding me so tight
I can't breathe.

He whispers in my ear, "You're such
a sexy Little Red Riding Hood."

He growls softly and nips at my neck.
A chill runs up my spine.

And the whole time, he's dancing me
closer and closer to the back door,

telling me that as soon as this song ends
he's going to whisk me away from here.

"Then we'll have three whole hours
to be alone together," he says.

"And the Halloween dance
will be your alibi."

The Second the Music Stops

Luke tugs me
toward the exit.

I try to pull his fingers off my wrist,
but his grip is like a handcuff.

"But I . . . I just got here," I say.
"I don't want to leave yet."

"You'll have even more fun," he says,
"where *we're* going."

"Where *are* we going?" I ask,
trying to keep the wobble out of my voice.

"It's a secret," he says,
shoving open the door.

I take one last glance
back over my shoulder,

hoping that I'll see my friends
rushing to my rescue.

But I don't see
Taylor or Rose anywhere.

And I don't see the woodcutter either.

We're Driving Through the Dark Streets

Jazz oozing out of the speakers,
when I get the first text:
Hey Lil. Where r u?
Tay n me can't find u anywhere.
"Who's it from?" Luke asks.

"Rose," I say. "She and Taylor
want to know where I am."
"Well, tell them . . . tell them
you got food poisoning," he says.
"Tell them your mom came and got you."

So I do—because if I told them the truth,
it'd probably wreck the dance for them.
But then, a few minutes later,
my phone buzzes again.
Luke shoots me a look.

This one's from Presley:
Rose says ur sick. Anything I can do?
"Who is it this time?" Luke snaps.
"Oh, it's just . . . just my friends again.
They're worried about me."

Luke drums his fingers on the steering wheel.
Then suddenly, they shoot out
and snatch the phone from my hand.
He switches it off
and slips it into his pocket.

My Blood Freezes

But I don't want him to know how scared I am.
So I hiss, "Turn this car around, Luke.
I'm not going anywhere with you."
He pulls over to the curb and reaches for my hand.

"Please don't be angry, Lily.
It's just that I wanted this night to be . . .
to be so romantic . . . Like one of those love
stories you're always reading . . . I wanted—"

Then his voice cracks,
and he doesn't finish his sentence.
His lower lip quivers,
like he's on the verge of tears.

Now I sort of feel like crying too.
"Oh, that's okay, Luke," I say.
"I'll bring you back to the dance now," he says.
"But can we just make one little stop first?"

I hesitate.
"Please," he begs, his voice trembling.
"There's something I really need
to show you."

Then he flashes me the saddest,
most heart-piercingly beautiful smile.
"Okay," I say, swallowing hard.
"One little stop."

Twenty Minutes Later

We park in front of a building
in a really seedy neighborhood.
There's two drunk guys
swearing at each other on the steps.

Luke takes my hand
and leads me past them,
then down a long corridor that smells
of stale cigarettes and grease.

He stops
in front of a scuffed-up metal door.
He unlocks it and shoves it open
with the toe of his boot.

Then he turns to me and says, "Ladies first."
I enter, and he flips the lock behind us.
The hairs on the back of my neck rise.
I glance around the small, dimly lit room.

There's only a stained gray love seat,
a lamp with a torn shade on a beat-up end table,
and a thin vase with a single
bright red lily in it.

"What do you think?" he asks.
"I . . . I dunno," I say. "What do *you* think?"
"I think it's a dump," he says with a grin.
"But it's *my* dump. I signed the lease this morning."

A Shudder Runs Through Me

"But . . . But don't you want
to live in a nicer apartment?" I ask.
"Don't be daft," he laughs.
"I'm not going to live here."

Then, as he pulls out a couple of candles
from a cabinet in the tiny kitchen alcove,
and starts lighting them, he adds, "This is just
a place where you and I can be alone."

He says he chose it because
the neighborhood is so sketchy
no one we know
ever comes down here.

He says that he can "tutor" me here,
and nobody will catch us coming and going.
That it will be lovely,
once he fixes it up.

That we'll have much more privacy here
than in that study room at the university.
"And we'll need it," he says.
"We can't do what *I* have in mind

in a room with no lock on the door."

My Heart Flings Itself Against My Ribs

Well, at least there's no bed, I'm thinking.
Not much can happen if there's no bed.

And just then,
he reaches for a handle on the wall

and yanks down
a hidden Murphy bed.

"Ta-da!" he says,
flashing me a hungry smile.

"I put pink satin sheets on it.
Just for you."

I want to tell him to take me home—
to take me home *right now*.

But when I open my mouth to speak,
the words refuse to come.

He Unties the Bow at the Neck of My Cape

He lifts it off my shoulders,
and lets it drop to the floor.

His eyes burn
as he looks me up and down.

Suddenly
I'm wishing I hadn't worn

such a clingy top . . .
such a short skirt . . .

I reach up and wipe away
the bead of sweat

that's rolling down
the side of my face.

And That's When I Notice

The two wineglasses
on the kitchen counter.

Luke pulls a bottle of champagne
from the fridge.

"Time to celebrate!" he says.
But I've never felt *less* like celebrating.

He puts his hand on the small of my back
and steers me over to the bed.

Then he lowers himself onto it
and pats the spot next to him.

"Join me," he says, his eyes glinting
like an animal's in a nightmare.

"I'm good,"
I manage to say.

But he takes hold of my hand
and pulls me down.

Luke Pours Two Glasses of Champagne

Then he gives me one,
and clinks his against mine.
"To us," he says.
"I . . . I don't want any," I say.

"But this is the best there is," he says.
His mouth is smiling, but his eyes aren't.
He guides my glass up to my lips.
"I don't want any," I repeat.

I try to turn my face away,
but he catches my chin in his hand.
"Please, Lily," he says.
"Don't ruin this special night for us."

I think about bolting for the door.
But it's almost as scary out there
as it is in here.
And Luke still has my phone.

I have no choice—so I choke down a sip.
It's bitter, but not as bad as beer.
He starts rubbing my shoulders.
"Have another sip, Lily," he says.

So I have
a little more.
And then, at his urging,
a little bit more . . .

I'm Feeling So Light-Headed Now

The room's blurring around me,
like I'm riding a merry-go-round
that's spinning way too fast.

I'm so dizzy I have to lie down.
I shut my eyes and let myself drift a little
on the satin sheets . . .

Then Luke's lips
are brushing across my forehead . . .
my lashes . . . my cheeks . . .

And now he's pressing them to mine . . .
Gently . . . So gently . . .
Like the very first time we kissed . . .

I feel
Luke's hands
drifting over my shoulders . . .

I feel
Luke's hands
gliding along my thighs . . .

I feel
Luke's hands
sliding up under my skirt!

My Eyes Pop Open

The champagne
lurches
in my stomach.
I try to push
his hands away,
but suddenly
my panties
are around my
ankles
and I'm struggling
to sit up,
but he's easing
down onto me,
pinning me under
the crushing dead weight
of his body.

He Starts Fumbling with His Fly

Tugging at his jeans and
everything's happening
way too fast and
now his cold hands
are on my knees and
he's trying to spread
my legs apart but
I'm clamping them together,
clawing at his fingers,
trying to pry them off me, and
all the while
he's kissing my neck,
murmuring,
"Come on, Lily.
You want this.
You know you do.
I've waited so long for you.
I can't wait a minute more.
I love you . . .
I love you so much."

And That's When

I hear the three voices—

the voices
of my heart
and my mind
and my body.

And all of them
are screaming

just
one
word.

"Nooooo!"

It's so earsplitting
it shocks Luke
into pulling back.

And the second he does
I slam both fists into his chest
and shove him off me.

Then I leap up
from the bed but
he grabs my wrist
and yanks me back down
and now his arms are closing
around me
and every muscle in my body
is tensing,
bracing
for what's coming
next.

And Then—

He starts crying.

Sobbing,
really.

Like
he's the most
miserable man
in the world.

He's Telling Me He's Sorry

He's so, so sorry.

And then I'm crying too,
and he's wiping away my tears
with his thumbs and we're looking
into each other's eyes.

But as I stare into his,
something slowly comes
into sharp focus.

It's like I'm seeing Luke
through the lens of my camera
and his secret is finally being revealed—
something is *missing* there.

Something is off.
Way off.

He's looking into my eyes,
but he's not seeing *me*—

all he's seeing
is his own reflection.

That's the only thing
he cares about—

himself.

That's All He's Ever Cared About

Suddenly,
I feel emptier
than a swimming pool
that's been drained for the winter.

We may
be crying together.

But we are crying
for two very different reasons.

And When Both of Us

Are finally all cried out,
he says he never meant to hurt me.
He says he'd never do *anything* to hurt me.

But he says we've been taking things so slow.
So slow it's killing him.

He says he knows I'm inexperienced
and he respects that and he's tried to be patient.
But he's a man, not a boy.
And a man reaches a point
when he needs more.

And he says
if I'm not able to give that to him,
he'll understand.
He will.

But if that's what I decide,
it'll just be impossible.
Impossible for him to bear.
So he'll have no choice.
No choice but to pack up his things
and move someplace far, far

away.

He Pauses Then

As if he's waiting
for me to say something.

And that's when
it dawns on me:

He's expecting me
to beg him to stay.

Even
after everything
that's just happened.

He's expecting me
to tell him I can't live
without him.

But that
is the opposite
of how I feel.

So I look him
right in the eye
and say,

"Then I guess it would be best
if you *did* leave town."

Luke Stares at Me Like He Can't Believe His Ears

He squeezes his dark eyes closed.
And when he opens them again,
a few seconds later,
he sighs a sigh deeper than a bottomless pit.

Then he puts his hands on my cheeks,
cradling my face in his palms,
and says he doesn't think I understand
what he's saying.

He doesn't think I realize
that if he's forced to move away,
forced to break every tie
with me and my family,
he'll have to take all his money
out of my father's business.

And he'd hate to have to do that.
He really would.

"Because if I do . . . ," he whispers,
pressing his forehead against mine.
"If I do . . .

your family will go bankrupt."

His Words

Are chains,
binding my clenched fists together.

His words are a jail cell,
its walls closing in
around me.

Luke has locked me up
with his words

and
swallowed
the
key.

How Could I Ever Have Loved This Man?

There's a stone in my chest
where my heart once was.

I imagine the look
on my parents' faces
when Luke tells them
he's taking his money back.

I see our house—an eviction notice
plastered across the front door,
all our stuff boxed up on the lawn
with nowhere to go.

I see Taylor and Rose and Presley,
standing on the sidewalk,
not knowing what to say to me.

I see Alice,
sitting on one of the boxes,
rocking back and forth
with her arms wrapped around herself,
her eyes lifeless and lost.

I could save myself.
But at what cost?

Then

I feel
Luke's lips
on my neck again.

And this time,
when he places
his icy fingers
onto my knees

I don't
even try
to pry them off . . .

When We Get Home

And Luke and I
walk through the front door,
my parents are right there
waiting for us.

They thank Luke
for picking me up from the dance.
He says it was no trouble at all.

My parents ask me
if I had a good time.
I say I did.

Why can't they see?
Why can't they see
what's happened to me?

Shouldn't
they know?

Doesn't it show?

I Force a Smile onto My Face

And tell them the dance was awesome,
carefully avoiding eye contact with Luke.

I make just enough small talk
to keep my parents from getting suspicious.
Then I say good night, rush up the stairs,
lock myself into my room,
and collapse against the door.

I reach up and grab hold
of Luke's tsavorite necklace.
It feels like a noose, strangling me.
I yank on it with both hands,
sending a shower of green stones
skittering across the floor.

Then I race to my closet
and get out my stepladder.
I climb to the top,
reach up to the ceiling,
and start tearing off
the glow-in-the-dark stars.

I scratch at them till my fingernails
are nothing but broken nubs,
and every single one of those stars

has been obliterated.

Later

I lie on my bed,
imagining what would happen
if I told my father
what Luke did to me.

I picture the color fading from his face.
I picture him grabbing the Maasai spear
from the hall closet—
the one that Luke brought him
from Kenya.

I picture him raging up the stairs with it,
the booming echo of his feet
making it sound like whole worlds
are being trampled beneath them.

I picture myself
dashing up the stairs behind him
and watching as he kicks open Luke's door.
I picture Luke's eyes widening
when he looks up and sees
the spear in my father's hand.

I picture the bursting out of the blood,
like a sudden blooming star on his chest,
and the terror and relief
spreading all through me
like the deep red puddle that's spreading
on the carpet at Luke's feet.

And Then

I picture my mother.
And Alice.

I picture them rushing into the room
at the sound of my shrieks.
I picture the squad cars
screeching up to our house.
And I picture my father's face—
strangely expressionless now,
like a blank sheet of paper.

I picture the police
exploding into the room
with their guns drawn.
And as they lead my father away,
I picture the look on Alice's face
and on my mother's—
like they're watching a horror film
that they can't turn off.

I picture all of this,
and I know beyond a shadow of a doubt,
that I can never *ever*

tell my father about Luke.

And I Can't Tell Mom Either

Because she'll tell Dad.
Even if I beg her not to.

And then,
even if he doesn't kill Luke,
he'll definitely send him away.

And if he sends Luke away,
he'll take his money with him
and then my father's company
will be wrecked,
and my mother will be so demolished
by everything that's happened,
she'll be too depressed to go to work.

And before we know it,
the four of us will be sleeping
in our SUV.

And then what?

Then what?

If Only

If only I hadn't
been such an awful flirt
that day Luke took Alice and me
to the beach.

If only I hadn't tickled him
and gazed into his eyes like I did
when we were playing in the waves.

If only I'd pulled away
when he leaned in to kiss me
that first time—

none of this
would be happening.

It's all
my fault.

All of it.

What I *Should* Have Done:

I should have listened
to Taylor and Rose when they
warned me about Luke.

I should have ended it
that day he carried me
to the couch,
unzipped his fly,
and pressured me
to do that stuff to him.
Even though he knew
I didn't want to.

I should have realized
right then and there
how sick that move was.
How sick *he* was.

But now—
it's too late.
I'm
in
way
over
my
head.

I'm drowning.
And no one can save me.

I've Been Trying to Sleep for Hours

I keep closing my eyes.
But they keep springing back open—
like one of Alice's ballerina dolls.

Finally, I sigh,
switch on the light,
and reach for *Rebecca*.
Maybe if I read for a while . . .

But when I open it
to the bookmarked page,
a shower of dried white lily petals
flutters out into my lap.

The petals from one of the lilies
Luke gave to my mom.

I'd forgotten
they were here.

I gather up every last one of them.
Then I rush to the bathroom,
fling them into the toilet,

and flush.

On Sunday

I tell my parents
I'm working on a school project,
and hide out in my room all day.

Presley calls.
But when I see his name on my screen,
my throat closes up
and I let it go straight to voice mail.

I can't even bring myself to listen
to the message he leaves.

A few minutes later,
Rose calls to ask
if I'm feeling well enough
to come to lunch with everyone
before Evan heads to the airport.
I tell her I'd love to,
but I'm still too sick to my stomach.

Which is the first time
I've told Rose the truth
in a very long while.

Then I hear everyone
shouting in the background.
"We love you, Lil. Feel better soon!"

But I can't imagine ever feeling better.

Later

Alice knocks on my door
and asks me if she can help me
with my project.

I thank her.
But I tell her
that this is something
no one
can help me with.

She cocks her head to the side.
"How come your eyes look so sad?" she asks.
"Oh . . . ," I say. "Just teenage stuff."
"I'll understand when I'm older?" she says.
"I'm afraid so," I say.

"Then I think I'll stay young
as long as I can," she says.
"That is an excellent plan," I say.

And I pull her into a hug,
blinking back tears.

At School the Next Morning

It's like I'm having
an out-of-body experience—
drifting along above myself,

watching as I wade through the halls
to get to chemistry,
like I'm slogging through mud,

watching the look of concern
that springs into Taylor's eyes
when he sees me come in,

watching him
put his hand on my arm and say,
"You look like death, Lil.
You sure you're over your food poisoning?"

Then watching myself force a smile,
and tell him it was really bad
for a while.

But that everything
is fine now.

Everything. Is. Fine.

In Creative Writing

Mr. Bennett says
we have to write haikus—

haikus that condense
how we're feeling
into seventeen syllables.

Here is mine:

Life sucks. Life sucks. Life
sucks. Life sucks. Life sucks. Life sucks.
It sucks . . . sucks . . . sucks . . . sucks.

In French Class

I slip into the room
a few minutes late
and collapse onto my seat.

Rose takes one look at me,
then reaches over to squeeze my hand
and whispers,
"*Etes-vous* okay, *ma chère Liliette?*"

"*Elle est une* total zombie today,"
Taylor whispers. "But she won't admit it."

Then he flashes me
such a worried, supportive smile
that I almost start crying—

right then and there,
in front of *tout le monde*.

And Lunch Isn't Any Easier

The second we sit down,
Taylor and Rose ask me what's up.
"And by 'What's up?'" Taylor says, "we mean
'Did you really have food poisoning?
Or did you leave the dance for . . .
for some other reason?'"

"You're scaring us," Rose says.
"You gotta tell us what's wrong.
It's a need-to-know situation."

I swallow the huge lump in my throat
and tell them nothing is wrong.

They exchange a glance,
and then Taylor says,
"Why can't you just admit
that this is about that older guy?"
"It's not about him," I say,
my voice cracking.

Though I can tell
that *they* can tell
it's totally about him.

So

We have
this weird silent conversation
with our eyes.

Because none of it
can be spoken out loud.

Since even
if they promised not to tell,
once they heard my secret,
they'd say *some* promises
need to be broken.

They'd say
they *have* to tell.

They'd say
it was for my own good.

But what about the good of my family?
I can't risk ruining all *their* lives
just because *I* made

a horrible mistake.

In Geometry

How can I be expected
to grasp the function rule,
when I can barely even function?

How can I concentrate
on trapezoids,
when I'm feeling
so totally trapped?

What's the point of studying rays,
when there's not a single ray of hope

on my horizon?

In Photography

Mr. Lewis spends the whole period
talking about self-portraits.

Presley keeps smiling at me,
trying to catch my eye.
But I pretend I don't notice.

Mr. L says cell phone selfies
aren't self-portraits.
They're junk food.

He says selfie sticks
should only be used
for one thing: kindling.

He says a real self-portrait
requires a shutter release or a mirror.
An actual mirror, not the ones in our phones.

He says a great self-portrait
shows us what's going on
on the surface
and below the surface too.
It reveals something
about the photographer
that no one else can reveal.

"The best self-portraits tell us the truth," he says,
"the whole truth, and nothing but the truth."

Homework Assignment: Self-Portrait

I hold my camera just below my chin,
aim it at the bathroom mirror,
and snap a picture of my reflection.

But when I look at it,
I see the truth
written all over my face—
in the dull staring eyes,
in the dark shadows below them,
in the grim straight line of my mouth.

So, of course,
I've got to delete it.

Suddenly I remember
my photo shoot with Presley,
and start leafing through *People* magazine.

I find a photo of a smiling model,
tear out the lips,
and tape them over my mouth.

Then I slip on my sunglasses,
and shoot a second self-portrait.

I check it,
to make sure the truth is hidden.
And decide that *this* one
is safe to send to Mr. L.

On Wednesday After School

Luke arranges to "tutor" me again.
He opens the door of the sleazy apartment.
He motions for me to enter before him
and says, "Ladies first."
Because he is *such* a gentleman.

He takes off his jacket
and helps me off with mine.
The lily is still in the thin vase.
But now its head is bent,
its petals the color of dried blood.

Luke kisses me.
Hard.
Though not so hard
that I'll look like I've been kissed.

Then he smiles a terrible smile,
and pulls the Murphy bed down from the wall.
I see the pink satin sheets and clench my teeth.

Luke says he needs me.
He says he wants me.
He says I'm his dream come true.

And I can almost remember back
to a time when I used to feel
the same way about him.

That Night

I'm curled up on my bed,
thinking about the leopard—
the one that Luke shot
after it sank its teeth into his arm.

I'm thinking about that leopard.
About how close it came
to killing him that day.

And about how different
my life would have been

if only
it had succeeded.

And when I hear Luke
tapping on my wall,

I don't tap back.

Now

Each "tutoring" session
is a torture session.

I try desperately to improve
my chemistry grade,
so my parents will finally call Luke off.
But I can't seem to raise it
any higher than a C.

I can't grasp liquid states
or solid states or *any* states.
Even when Taylor explains them to me.
In fact, I'm having trouble
in *all* my classes.

I guess it's hard to do well in school
when you can't even think straight.

And it's hard to think straight
when you're not getting any sleep.

And it's hard to sleep
when you're plagued
by headaches so horrible
that whenever you close your eyes
you feel like there's an ax in your head—

an ax that's trying to hack its way out
through the walls of your skull.

At School

Madame Melvoin says she's *très perplexe*
about my *mauvaises* grades.
She asks me how things are *chez moi*.
"*Ça va . . . bien*," I tell her.
She raises an eyebrow and says, "*Oui?*"
"*Oui*," I say.

And Ms. Peyser
has noticed something's up too.
Or maybe she just feels sorry for me.
Because she offers to let me
take my chemistry test over,
to try and bring my grade up.
I take it again,
but I don't do any better.

Even Mr. Bennett has gotten suspicious.
He passes back my poetry quiz
(which I barely managed to get a B- on)
with a little note that says:
I'm here every day after school,
if you feel like chatting.

I do not feel like chatting.

Especially Not with My Parents

But they come up to my room
one night after dinner
and tell me they're worried about me—
about my falling grades, my weight loss,
the circles under my eyes.

They tell me
they don't know what's going on,
but they hate to see me struggling like this
and they want to help.

I'm too worn out
to make something up.
So I decide to tell them the truth.

I tell them
I was in love with a guy.

But he broke my heart.

My Mother Hugs Me

My father pats my shoulder.
Then they offer to send me
to a therapist.

But I tell them I don't need one.
I tell them I'll get over it.
I just need a little time.

But in my head
I'm thinking:

A little time
or a little good luck—
like Luke getting struck by lightning.

"Well, Lilybelle," Dad says,
and my throat instantly closes up,
because he never calls me that.
"There's only ten days till Thanksgiving.
You'll get some rest over the nice long weekend,
and it will help heal that heart of yours."

I lean my head against his chest
and let the tears fall.

Later That Night

I hear a quiet knock on my door.
A wave of nausea grips me.
Is it Luke?

But then I hear Alice's voice.
"Can I come in?"

I open the door and there she is—
her chubby fingers wrapped around
the handle of a wrinkled orange paper bag
filled with what must be the last
of her Halloween stash.

"You've been looking a little . . .
a little hungry lately," she says shyly.
Then she reaches into the bag,
pulls out a handful of Hershey's Kisses,
and offers them to me.
"Look!" she says. "Your favorite."

"*You're* my favorite," I say.
And I bury my face in her silky curls.

I Wade Through the Next Week and a Half

In constant dread
of each "tutoring" session,
                feeling as if my body
        has been drained
of all its blood,
        and in its place
                is a swarm of tiny bees,
        circling endlessly
through my veins,
        relentlessly flapping
                their tiny bee wings,
                buzzing,
                buzzing,
        buzzing,
                till I want
                        to unzip my
                                vibrating
                        skin
                and let
                        them
                                all fly
                                out.

The Day Before Thanksgiving Break

Mr. L asks me to stay after class.
We sit facing each other across his desk.
He studies me, then clears his throat
and tells me he's noticed a change
in the quality of my work lately.
I can feel my cheeks blaze up.
I say I'm sorry. I say I'll try to do better.
I say I've been a little distracted lately.

But he smiles at me and tells me
I've misunderstood—he loves my stuff.
He's never seen such honest student work.
"That self-portrait," he continues.
"The one you submitted a few weeks ago.
It's haunted me. It was so . . . so revealing."
Damn. It was supposed to be
the opposite of revealing.

"But it made me wonder," he says,
"if there's anything more you'd like to reveal.
I mean, to me. In complete confidence, of course."

My chest aches.
I yearn to tell him everything.
But I can't take that chance.
Besides, Luke will be waiting for me.
He doesn't like it when I'm late.
So I say, "Not really. But thanks, Mr. L."
Then I bolt from the room.

And Run Right into Presley

He must have been waiting for me.
I try to slip past him,
but he steps in front of me.
He says, "Is everything okay, Lil?"
He looks so concerned I can't bear it.
I swallow hard and say, "Sure."

But he puts his hands on my shoulders and says,
"You told me you wanted to be friends, right?"
I nod, biting my lip to keep it from quivering.
"Well, as your friend," he says,
"I can see something's wrong.
Let me help you, Lil.
Let a friend help a friend."

I meet his gaze, but I know
if I say anything I'll tear up.
So I wrap my arms around him,
just for a second,
thinking that if things had been different
maybe we would have been able
to be more than friends.
So much more.

Then I pull away, run down the corridor,
and out the door—

into Luke's waiting car.

Thanksgiving Dinner

Luke
has taken
the seat next to mine.

He's toasting my parents,
clinking his wineglass against theirs,
his other hand stroking my thigh
under the tablecloth.

I can't think
of a single thing
I'm thankful for.

I've Been Avoiding Taylor and Rose

Sending their calls to voice mail.
Ignoring their texts.
Skipping every sleepover.

But on Saturday afternoon,
they show up at my door
and tell me they're kidnapping me.

I say I have too much homework.
They tell me it's Thanksgiving break
and that I need to *take* one.

I say I'm coming down with a cold.
They tell me they'll make me some turkey soup.

I say I'm not fit for human consumption.
They tell me to just shut up already
and come with them.

Even my parents are in favor
of me getting out of the house.
They practically shove us out the door,
and call after us to have fun.

Fun? Fun . . .
Isn't that that thing
I used to have all the time?
That thing I took for granted?

But When Rose's Brother Drops Us Off

I realize we're at Looking Glass Lanes.
And suddenly I'm flashing back
to when Luke took Alice and me here,
remembering exactly how I felt that day—
like everywhere was Wonderland
when I was with Luke.
It seems so long ago.
As if those feelings belonged to a stranger.

I choose a ball with flames painted all over it.
I heave it up till it's just below my chin.
I stare down the lane,
imagining that the center pin is Luke.
Then I hurl the ball, and—*strike!*
Rose and Taylor clap and cheer.

When my second turn comes,
I imagine I'm aiming right at Luke's crotch . . .
And—*strike!*
Rose and Taylor scream and high-five me.

When my third turn comes,
I hold that same thought, and—*strike!*
They shriek and jump up and down.
"Whoa," Taylor says. "We wouldn't
have invited you if we knew you'd win."

Wait. What's this odd sensation?
Oh. Now I remember—*this* is fun.

After That

They don't even have to talk me into
sleeping over at Rose's.
I'm totally on board.

And for the next few hours,
while the Triatomics bake cupcakes,
and do each other's nails,
and watch an old movie on TV,

I don't even *think* about Luke.

But in the Morning

It all comes crashing back down
over me.

It turns out Taylor and Rose
both have family stuff planned.
But I don't want to call home for a ride,
because they might send Luke.
So I catch the bus home.

I'm sitting in the back,
trying not to think, trying not to feel,
when I notice this guy staring at me—

staring right at me with dead black eyes,
licking his lips as if he'd rather
be licking mine.

I turn my head away
and squeeze my eyes closed.

But I can still see those eyes.
Those dead black eyes.

There's something
all too familiar about them.

When I Walk into the House

I hear Alice giggling.
I look into the living room.
She's sitting on the couch next to Luke.
They don't notice me standing here.

His arm is around her shoulder.
Her favorite ballerina book
is resting on his knees.
Luke's reading it to her.

At the end of each page,
Alice reaches over into his lap
to turn to the next one,
and then to the next.

And my stomach twists
and twists again.

When they finish the book,
Alice throws her arms around his neck,
beams up at him, and says,

"I'm gonna marry you when I grow up."

And When Luke

Smiles
down at her,

and
promises
he'll wait
for her,

I break out
into a cold sweat.

I Back Away

Then I turn
and stagger out the door.

I rush down
the front walk,

and when I reach the road,
I start running—

I run as if
my whole life
depends on it.

As if
Alice's whole future
depends on it.

As if
a wolf is chasing me,
snarling and snapping
at my heels.

My Feet Fly Over the Pavement

I don't even know
where I'm headed.

All I know is—
I have to get there.

I run and run and run,
and as I do,
I'm thinking about Alice.

Thinking about
how much I love her.
And about how sweet she is.
And how innocent.

Just as innocent
as *I* was—

when I used to fling my arms
around Luke's neck

and say those
very same words.

My Churning Thoughts

Fall into rhythm
with my pounding feet.

I've got to
do something . . .
do something . . .
do something . . .

Because
if I don't,

someday
Luke will destroy
Alice's life—

just like
he has destroyed
mine.

And I can't
let that happen to her.

I can't.

Nothing
else matters.

Nothing but Alice.

Suddenly

I know
where I'm going.

And I start running
even faster.

I run
till it feels

like there's a knife
digging into my side,

and my
calves burn,

and my breath
is coming in short

sharp
gasps.

But

I keep
right on
going

and
I don't
stop

till
I reach
Bella's.

I Peer Through the Window

And when
I see Bella,
sitting behind the counter,

her head
bent over
an open book,

a wave of relief
crests over me,
then floods all through me.

And as it does, my stone heart
softens and starts beating again—
its hopeful rhythm filling my chest.

I take
a minute
to catch my breath.

Then
I reach for the handle,
yank open the heavy oak door,

and
    step
        inside.

Bella Looks Up

She hurries over to me,
the tiny bells in her skirt tinkling,

and gathers me
into a hug.

"My darling," she says.
"I've been expecting you."

I rest my head
against her strong shoulder,

and inhale that comforting
dust-and-books-and-cookies smell.

Then I say,
"I need your help."

Author's Note

In this story, when Luke sexually abuses Lily, she thinks it is all her fault. But Lily is one hundred percent wrong about that. If someone forces you to do anything sexual that you don't want to do, it's never your fault. It doesn't matter if you flirted with them. It doesn't matter if you kissed them, or didn't stop them in the beginning. If you change your mind and want to stop at any point, the other person must honor your request. If they won't stop when you ask them to, that is not okay.

In addition to sexually abusing Lily, Luke also sexually coerces her. He says he will ruin her family financially if she doesn't have sex with him. When someone says you have to do something sexual that makes you uncomfortable, and claims there will be negative consequences if you refuse, that's sexual coercion. And it is not okay.

Unwanted sexual behavior is never okay—whether the person is much older than you are, as is the case with Luke and Lily, or the same age as you, or even younger. It doesn't matter whether the person is a stranger, someone you are dating, a friend, a family member, or someone you or your family knows and trusts, like it is in Lily's situation. It is totally unacceptable. And it is definitely not your fault.

When Lily asks Bella for help, she is starting a chain of events that will lead to Luke getting arrested and receiving the punishment he deserves. If you or someone you know is ever sexually abused, please don't wait as long as Lily waited to seek help. Get help right away. Tell your parents, another relative, one of your friend's parents, a clergy member, or a teacher. And if you ever find yourself in immediate danger, call 911.

You are not alone. There *is* a way out!

HERE ARE SOME ORGANIZATIONS THAT CAN HELP:

NATIONAL SEXUAL ASSAULT HOTLINE
800-656-HOPE (4673)

If you have been raped, or if you want to talk to someone anonymously about the sexual abuse that is happening to you or to a friend, or even if you are unsure that what you are experiencing *is* sexual abuse, you can call this number 24 hours a day and be put through to the nearest sexual assault service provider.

RAPE, ABUSE & INCEST NATIONAL NETWORK (RAINN)
www.rainn.org

RAINN is the largest anti-sexual-violence organization in the United States. Their website is excellent and will help you find the help you need. You can chat online anonymously with someone in English or Spanish 24/7 at www.rainn.org/get-help.

LOVEISRESPECT
www.loveisrespect.org

Loveisrespect's purpose is to empower teens to prevent and end abusive relationships. Highly trained advocates offer support, information, and advocacy to teens who have questions or concerns about their dating relationships. They also provide information and support to concerned friends. You can chat with them online 24/7. Confidential phone and texting services are also available. Call 866-331-9474 or text loveis to 22522.

There is a special section of the Loveisrepect website geared toward members of the LGBTQ community: http://www.loveisrespect.org/is-this-abuse/abusive-lgbtq-relationships/.

BREAK THE CYCLE
www.breakthecycle.org

Break the Cycle inspires and supports young people 12–24 to build healthy relationships. They are a culturally affirming, diverse organization that believes all young people deserve to live in a world where they can thrive.

Acknowledgments

Writing this book was the opposite of easy. There are many kind and generous people I'd like to thank for helping me along the way:

My brilliant editor, Alexandra Cooper, who never stopped asking just the right questions.

My inspired and hardworking HarperCollins team, who did more than I will ever know: Rosemary Brosnan, Alyssa Miele, Catherine San Juan, Olivia Russo, Bess Braswell, and Ebony LaDelle.

My jeweler, FashionLILLA, who created the perfect necklace for the cover, and Michael Frost, who photographed it so beautifully.

My critique group members, Ann Wagner Wilson and Betsy Rosenthal Rosenthal, who hung in there, week after week, listening to this hard-to-listen-to story and helping me make it better.

My agent, Steven Malk, who was always there for me, working his magic behind the scenes.

My sweet Thirds, who buoyed me up with their monthly dose of much needed sisterly support.

Richard Peck, who invited me to read aloud a short stack of early pages. I heard your voice in my head while I wrote every page that followed.

Gilda Frantz, the wisest woman I know, who kept me afloat through the worst of the storm.

My daughter, Ava, who suggested I write this book quickly. At first I laughed—as if such a thing could be done! And then I thought, "Why not?"

My son, Jeremy, who pointed out that there really wasn't **any** reason not to keep right on running till I reached THE END.

My husband, Bennett, who held my hand and my **heart** throughout the journey.

And my poetry teacher, Myra Cohn Livingston, who set me **on** the path before I even knew it was there.

Don't miss SAVING RED, a powerful
novel in verse about the meaning of home,
from acclaimed author Sonya Sones.

Why Am I Out Here

In the middle of the freaking night
wandering the streets of Santa Monica
looking for homeless people

when I could be lying in bed
watching videos of babies eating lemons
and soldiers reuniting with their dogs?

Because I need four more hours
of community service this semester.
That's why.

And
I need them
by tomorrow morning.

I Know, I Know

I shouldn't have waited
till the very last minute.

But isn't that what
the very last minute is for?

I mean, if God hadn't wanted us
to wait until the very last minute,

he wouldn't have
created it, right?

Unfortunately

This morning, when I explained
that theory to my Freshman Seminar teacher,
she just laughed and said,

"Molly, if God hadn't
wanted us to meet deadlines,
she wouldn't have created them.

And you've known for months now
that every student has to complete
their community service before winter break."

Which is why I am out here
freezing my butt off
at eleven thirty at night,

with a clipboard and a tally sheet
and a pen that only works
when you wring its neck,

roaming the streets
with my faithful dog Pixel
and 250 other volunteers—

all of us
helping the city
take its annual homeless count.

Which is sort of like
being on a scavenger hunt.
Only much less fun.

Not at *All* Fun, Actually

I mean,
I knew there were people
living on the streets in Santa Monica.
You'd have to be blind not to notice them.

Though until tonight
I never really focused on them.
In fact, I tried really hard
not to focus on them.

Whenever I saw someone sleeping in an alley
or picking through a trash can
or trudging along in taped-up shoes,
I looked away and hurried past them.

Not because I'm one of those
spoiled self-centered teenage girls
whose idea of unendurable hardship
is having a broken fingernail.

But because . . .
Well, because seeing those people
stirs up all sorts of stuff in me.
Stuff I don't like to think about.

Though Tonight

I *can't* look away
and hurry past them.
Because tonight it's my job
to count them for the city.

My mom never would've signed
the permission slip
if she knew I was doing this
alone.

I had to lie and tell her
some friends were coming with me.
Even though I have exactly
zero friends.

So the people running this event
assigned Pixel and me to a random team
with these two ancient hippies—
Feather and Eden.

Their clothes are so scruffy
they kind of look
a little homeless themselves.
But they're not so bad, I guess.

If you don't mind hanging out
with a couple of people
who've decided it's their mission in life
to convince you of the many joys

of a gluten-free
meat-free dairy-free
soy-free fish-free
free-free existence.

At First We Can't Find Any Homeless People

But when we get to Reed Park,
we spot a guy with a long white beard
wedged into the skinny plastic slide
for toddlers,

a baseball cap
covering his eyes,
his hands crossed over his chest
like a corpse in an open casket.

We stand here for a while,
just sort of watching him sleep.
And suddenly I've got this lump in my throat,
and I'm wishing we could help him somehow . . .

The event organizers
warned us we'd feel this way.
But they said we weren't allowed
to interact with the people we find.

They said we should just concentrate
on counting as many of them as we can.
Because the more people we count tonight,
the more homeless funding the city will get.

So I swallow hard,
mark the guy down on our tally sheet,
and force myself to follow
Feather and Eden out of the park.

We Head West on Wilshire Boulevard

And pretty soon we notice a man
sleeping on a bench at a bus stop,
cradling a suitcase held together
with duct tape and string.

And just as we cross over 5th Street,
we see a woman sleeping in a beat-up Toyota,
crammed full of all the stuff
that once must have been in her closet.

Then, a couple of blocks later, we see
an old woman dozing on a yoga mat
tucked underneath a stairwell,
her fingers gripping a mangy stuffed bear.

And when I see that shriveled old lady
clutching that bear, my heart shrivels too.
And it's all I can do to keep myself
from calling 911

and begging them
to get over here right now
and find her a place to live.
Find *all* these people places to live . . .

We've Been Scouring Our Assigned Area

For a couple of hours now,
on this totally strange,
totally sad search that we're on.
And I'm pretty sure I'm starting to get frostbite.

(I know this is
Southern California.
But when it dips into the forties here,
it feels colder than Alaska to *us*!)

I zip up my jacket
and pull my socks higher,
thinking that I can hardly wait
for these four hours to be over

so that I can slip into my pajamas,
climb into my nice warm bed,
cuddle up with Pixel,
and drift off to sleep . . .

But then I spot a young guy
sleeping in front of the Converse store,
wrapped up like a sausage in a moldy blanket,
his swollen bare feet sticking out at the bottom.

And all of a sudden
I'm blinking back tears.
Because seeing him
lying there like that makes me . . .

Makes me think about *another* young guy . . .

Suddenly

My fingers
start tingling . . .

There's a ringing in my ears . . .
I can't breathe . . . !

My chest—it's splitting in two!
I'm having a heart attack!

But then Pixel's here—
standing on his hind legs,

resting his soft white paws
against my thigh,

peering up at me through his shaggy bangs
as if to say, "Easy now, kiddo."

He nudges the comforting knob
of his nose into the palm of my hand,

reminding me that I'm just having
another panic attack—not a heart attack.

That all I need to do is take
some slow, deep breaths and I'll be fine.

I stroke his secret sweet spot,
right behind that floppy left ear of his,

and I can feel my teeth beginning to unclench,
my heart rate returning to normal.

What would I do without Pixel?